Snowed in on Main Street

ALSO BY KASEY STOCKTON

Contemporary Romance

Snowflake Wishes

Snowed In on Main Street

Melodies and Mistletoe

Cotswolds Holiday

Regency Romance

All is Mary and Bright

A Forgiving Heart

Sensibly Wed

Pleasantly Pursued

The Jewels of Halstead Manor

The Lady of Larkspur Vale

Love in the Bargain

Scottish Romance

Journey to Bongary Spring

Through the Fairy Tree

Snowed in on Main Street

KASEY STOCKTON

GOLDEN OWL PRESS

CHAPTER ONE

Mia Murphy pressed the phone to her ear and spoke to her boss in her most conciliatory tone. "I promise, everything will be fine. Enjoy the Arizona sun and don't even think twice about Powder Peaks again. We will be *fine*." Mia hung up the phone and sat against the counter, giving her friend and coworker, Ashlyn, a wide-eyed look of exasperation.

"Janice again?" Ashlyn asked, her nose wrinkling.

"Yes." Mia pressed her fingers to her temples. "I'm ready to run the hotel. I've been ready for months. She needs to take a deep breath and realize that everything will be—"

"Fine?" Ashlyn asked facetiously, pulling her frizzy red hair back into a scrunchy and lifting an eyebrow.

"As a matter of fact," Mia said, pushing away from the wall. "I believe it will be."

"Clearly." Ashlyn sat back in her chair behind the front desk and picked up a pen, chewing on the end of it. "I just couldn't figure out if you were convincing Janice of that or yourself."

Mia reached forward and pulled the pen away from Ashlyn's mouth, her friend's grin widening. "Professionally speaking, I'm sure everything will be great. Having to miss Christmas with my

1

family this year because I'm working the whole week...that part I'm not looking forward to as much. The sacrifice is worth the chance to prove myself though."

Ashlyn typed into the computer. "Well, if it's family time you're missing, you can live vicariously through the guests. We've got a family coming in tomorrow, and they've booked the Wasatch Room for holiday activities nearly every day."

Mia didn't want to sound like a know-it-all, so she let her friend continue. But she had gone over the guest list and general itinerary for the hotel at least a dozen times last week, making a special mental note of the important guests and their needs. They had one VIP coming for the week, and Mia was prepared.

This was her shot to prove to Janice she was capable of running the hotel and deserved the promotion to manager. The older woman had more and more reasons to miss work with her growing brood of grandchildren, and Mia knew she was the person for the job. She'd put in the work, and she cared about this hotel. It was about time.

Ashlyn continued, her eyebrows lifting as she spoke. "They will have the entire third floor, all four suites and one single room. And apparently coming to Powder Peaks Lodge is a tradition for them, so Janice added a few notes to the file of things you need to be aware of. I guess she gives them special treatment? They have a whole sugar cookie decorating event and we provide the sprinkles. And they have access to extra snowmobiles rented through Janice. It's a whole thing."

"Good to know." And good thing Mia already *did* know, or she'd be panicking right at that moment. "I better go double check all our vendor deliveries."

"Probably smart." Ashlyn popped a piece of gum into her mouth. "I think the first of the guests arrive tomorrow."

They *were* scheduled to arrive tomorrow. But Mia noticed a few of them had changed their reservations to tonight. She didn't bother correcting Ashlyn. She walked away, her low heels clicking softly down the wood plank floors. She let herself through the door that led down to the basement and picked up the clipboard hanging on the wall. She slid her finger down the columns until she found the deliveries that had arrived and been stored earlier that morning.

She could smell the laundry going on the other side of the room and nodded to herself. Things were falling into place. Up on the landing, she took the stairs toward the suites to check them again one final time.

Her phone buzzed halfway through her perusal and she slid it on, accepting the video call.

"Hey, Mom." Mia walked through the suite slowly, checking soaps and drinks and ensuring that nothing was left in the drawers by the previous occupants.

"Did you see the storm blowing your way?" Mom said, worry lacing her tone. "It already hit most of the Wasatch front, and it's confirmed to glide right through Park City."

Unease clenched her stomach. That was one thing Mia hadn't thought to check. "Shoot, no. How bad is it?"

Mom lifted her pale eyebrows, her lips closing into a thin line. That wasn't good. "I know the Powells had to cancel their trip to Montana because they couldn't get out of town."

"Maybe the storm left all its snow with you guys and will run out by the time it reaches me."

Mom didn't look convinced. "You have extra blankets, right? And what about a full supply of food? I don't like it that you're up that mountain road, Mia. If you lose electricity and get cut off from everything, that could get dangerous."

Mia gave her mom a reassuring smile. "I just triple checked our stores, and we have everything we need, even a backup generator. I think we'll be fine, no matter what happens." Right? She hoped so. "Besides, if it came to that, we've got a shed in the back with snowmobiles so someone could go for help. No one is dying up this mountain road, Mom, no matter how bad the storms get."

"I still don't understand why you can't find a nice resort to work at in Park City, instead of that tiny little mountain town. It's just so remote."

Mia closed her eyes. Mom made it sound like she was in the middle of nowhere, but she was only a few minutes up the road from Park City. She loved the lodge, and she loved her boss. Why work for a posh Park City resort when she could run a smaller hotel just up the road with such charm and charisma?

"I'm happy here," she said simply.

Mom was silent a moment before saying, "Listen, I know you can't make it home for Christmas this year, so I sent you a little something in the mail. Don't wait to open it."

"I won't." Mia let herself into the final room on the row and placed the phone on the counter facing her while she checked the bathrooms. "And I'll come home for a few days as soon as Janice returns from Arizona." She picked up the phone, looking at her mom to prove her sincerity. "I *am* sad to miss Christmas, but I really couldn't pass up this opportunity."

"I know, honey. I'm proud of you. I just wish you could be with us."

Mia placed the phone on the windowsill and checked the drawers beside the bed. "Hey, good thing I checked. I found a bouncy ball." She turned and held it up for her mom to see the tiny, hot pink rubber ball that had been left behind in the drawer. It slipped from her fingers and bounced, hitting the wall and rolling under the bed. She groaned.

"Dropped it?" her mom asked.

"Yes," Mia hollered, getting down on her belly to look under the bed. She grimaced. A hotel floor—even though she worked there and *knew* it was cleaned thoroughly and regularly—was not her favorite place to be. She spotted the ball near to the center of the giant king-sized bed and considered the merits of leaving it there.

The guests probably wouldn't have any idea it was there, and she could ask one of the housekeepers to fetch it out with a vacuum hose when they next cleaned.

But then the room wouldn't be perfect. And this week, *everything* needed to be perfect.

"You know," she heard her mom saying on the phone, "I think I saw Harold Schuman at the gas station the other day with Nancy Farr. I think they might be dating."

"Well, for a man of his age, all I have to say is good for them," Mia hollered back, her face pressed against the wooden floor.

"I thought the same thing," Mom said. "And I think if your dad was single at ninety-one and took a fancy to a nice woman, I wouldn't be mad if he started dating her."

"How magnanimous of you."

"Elliot James?" Mom said, loudly.

A ball of disgust formed in Mia's stomach, and her face fixed in a scowl. "Gross, Mom. I'm already lying on a hotel floor. Don't send me over the edge here or I'll lose my lunch."

"No, honey," her mom said. *"Elliot James."*

Mia lifted her head so her mom could hear her better from across the room. "I heard you the first time. Now I'm kind of glad I'm missing Christmas at home. I'd rather get run over by Santa's sleigh than see *him* again."

She stretched her fingers, their tips grazing the ball. Scooting further under the bed, she reached as far as she could and tapped the ball so it would roll out the other side.

"I mean, *really*. The guy is on every single channel lately. It makes me sick—"

A throat cleared inside the room, and Mia went cold.

She pushed herself out from under the bed, slowly lifted her head over the edge of the mattress, and stared straight into the gorgeous green eyes of Utah's sweetheart.

And her ex-boyfriend. Elliot James.

Blood pumped through her ears and her cheeks burned. Mom's voice sounded far away when she spoke. "I'll let you get back to work, honey. Nice to see you, Elliot."

"Nice to see you, too, Mrs. Murphy." Elliot's voice was just as deep as Mia remembered, and it ran through her veins like ice water.

But what was he doing here?

Elliot stood in the hotel room across from his ex-girlfriend and drank in the sight of her like rain after a drought. His heart rate increased as he took in her same blonde hair, same blue eyes, and her dainty little nose, regardless of the fact that it was scrunched up in disgust—because of him.

He allowed his mouth to form a small smile. His gaze drifted to her name tag and his eyebrows lifted accordingly. "Assistant manager? Nice."

Distaste brought her nose up even further. "We all can't be TV stars, you know."

"What?" She'd misunderstood him. "No. I meant it. It *is* nice."

She nodded slowly, and he could tell he wasn't making any headway there. He was usually so much smoother than this, but seeing her had been such a shock. He rubbed the back of his neck. "So, you'd rather get run over by a sleigh—"

"What are you doing here?" she said, her cheeks turning pink.

So joking wasn't the way to get into her good graces, either. "A family vacation."

"These suites are saved for the Caldwells."

"Yes," he agreed. "My mom's side."

Her eyes lit up with recognition. "Right. So...is your whole family coming?"

He glanced to the window and the snow steadily falling. He'd made it through Parley's Canyon safely but with the weather report playing on the driver's radio, he was wondering if his family would make it before the snow came.

"That's the plan," he said.

She brought her hands together in front of her in a businesslike pose and tilted her head. Her voice took on a robotic effect as she spoke. "Welcome to Powder Peaks Lodge. I won't bother introducing myself since you already know my name, but I will be Acting Manager during the course of your stay. Please do not hesitate to call down to the front desk or ask for me directly if there is anything you find yourself in need of."

She gave him a bright smile, but it didn't reach her eyes.

"Great," he said. He could tell she wanted to get away from him. But after six years, he was oddly reluctant to let her go.

Elliot stepped out of the pathway to the door to let her pass. And she did so with immense speed. No sooner had the door shut behind her, however, than a knock sounded on it.

He stepped forward and opened the door, his heart thrumming in his chest at her return.

"I left my phone," she said, indicating where it sat on the windowsill.

Elliot stepped out of her way and she retrieved her phone, giving him a wide berth as she sped past him again.

This was going to be an interesting week.

CHAPTER TWO

L ying flat on the rustic bed in the cabin-like room, Elliot
turned on his phone again, as if checking one more time
would bring in texts from his family. But nope. Still nothing.

He blew out a breath before rising and crossing to the
window. The view was nothing but snow-covered mountains
and the other side of Hidden Hollow's Main Street with its row
of buildings nestled together like they'd been squeezed and
squished into a mold. For such a tiny town, they had a decent
array of restaurants on their miniature Main Street, and Elliot
was looking forward to visiting some of them.

He loved coming to Hidden Hollow for Christmas each year
but passing through Park City to get there was bittersweet. The
Olympic rings on the flags everywhere were a bold reminder of
his failure.

Frustrated, he turned on his phone again and located his
mom's number. The call immediately failed. He moved it away
from his face and checked the corner, feeling like a complete
idiot when he noticed the tiny airplane symbol.

He'd forgotten to take his phone off airplane mode when his

flight landed. He switched it back to normal, and his phone immediately blew up with voicemails and texts from various people—family, friends, and coworkers.

Elliot opened his messages and scanned them quickly for pertinent information. He clicked the family chat and dread filled his body, slowly rising as he read more and more.

Messages back and forth between his parents—who were supposed to be carpooling with his grandparents—his older brother's family, and his aunt and uncle all described how they were stuck in one way or another. His brother was the last to text, explaining that he made it out of town but couldn't get through the canyon which led from his house to Park City.

The only person who was as silent in the messages as he had been was his sister, Amy.

He leaned back on the bed and dialed his mom's number again.

She picked up right away, her voice sounding anxious. "Elliot, sweetheart, did you make it to Utah?"

"Yes. Actually, I made it through Park City already."

She blew out a breath that filled his ear with static. "I wish I had the foresight to tell you to skip the lodge and travel straight home, but the roads are ice and there's no way you'd get through safely now."

"It's fine, Mom," he said, infusing his voice with more pleasantness than he felt. "I can stay here tonight and find a ride out of here tomorrow."

She was silent, and he chose not to read into her skepticism.

"Christmas is still four days away," he said. "A lot can change in that amount of time."

"True," she agreed. "And in the meantime, watch out for your sister. I've been calling her all day and haven't heard anything back."

"Okay, will do."

"I love you, Elliot."

He smiled, suddenly wishing for his Mom to be in the room with him where she could wrap him in a hug and make him feel better. He blinked. He hadn't wished for something so childish in a while.

Well, since the accident, at least.

He knew a desire for a moment to tell his mom who it was he'd seen crawling under his bed when he'd arrived at the hotel, but he didn't want her to worry more than she already was, so he kept it to himself.

"I love you too, Mom," he said, and hung up the phone.

Elliot stood and pulled out his wallet to tuck his room key inside. If he was going to be stuck in Hidden Hollow alone, he might as well have some good food to get him through the night.

"Ashlyn," Mia hissed, slapping her hands on the front desk. She was sure her eyes looked crazed, but she had no control over her emotions at present. She was doing her best not to implode.

The redhead lifted her gaze, worry evident in the widening of her eyes. "What's happened?"

"Elliot James is upstairs."

Ashlyn immediately relaxed, a grin spreading over her lips. "I know. I checked him in. Can you believe *Elliot James* is staying at our hotel? He's a day early, but I went back through Janice's notes and she amended the reservation a few days ago to say that he'd arrive today."

Mia leaned her elbows on the tall countertop and dropped her head in her hands. So *his* was the reservation which was arriving early. Why hadn't Janice written his name with it? It had simply said, *Caldwell VIP.* "That would have been nice to know."

"What happened?"

Mia peeked through her fingers. "I was checking out his room when he got there." She bared her teeth in a grimace. "And video chatting with my mom."

Ashlyn's face broke out in a grin.

Mia continued. "And of *all* the people—"

"Hello," a deep voice said from behind her. "Ashlyn, is it?"

Oh, you've got to be kidding me.

"Yes, Mr. James?" Ashlyn said, batting her eyelashes like a coquettish lady in a Jane Austen film.

Mia stepped away from the desk, waiting off to the side with her hands clasped in clenched fists behind her back.

Elliot focused on Ashlyn, offering her his winning smile. "If anyone else from my family arrives, will you tell them I'm just heading down to Hal's to grab a bite to eat?"

"Of course, Mr. James."

He casually slung his hands in his jeans pockets and dipped his head before leaving the lobby.

Mia began fanning her face with her hand. "Wow it's stuffy in here. What is the heat set to?"

"Seventy-one," Ashlyn said, giving her a side eye, "like always. Are you doing okay?"

"Yes," Mia answered right away. "I'm not overwhelmed. Just thrown off my equilibrium."

A woman stepped out of the elevator with a perfectly round, white head of hair, trailing her tiny dog behind her on a long, thin, red leash. Mia snapped to attention. "Hello, Mrs. Bruin. How are you enjoying your accommodations?"

"The room is just lovely, dear," Mrs. Bruin said as her terrier wandered toward the large Christmas tree set before the front windows. "I will be so sad to leave tomorrow."

"And we will be sad to see you leave. Is there anything I can do for you?"

"Not now. But maybe I'll call down a little later." Mrs. Bruin sent a wink and Mia smiled until the woman gathered her dog and left the building. Mrs. Bruin had called down for chocolate cake every evening since her arrival last week. They'd grown to expect the call right at eleven, sharp, every night. Mia had had to run out and get some for the older woman, because chocolate cake in the evening was not something they offered. But Mia wanted everything to be perfect while Janice was away.

Once the lobby was clear again, Mia turned to Ashlyn. "I'm going to find Marco to check on the backup generators."

Ashlyn saluted her and she left.

Marco was extremely helpful, locating the backup generators and explaining how they functioned. "They're already set up to kick in if the power ever goes out, so you don't need to panic. Who's on night shift tonight?"

"Me," Mia said. "I'm covering for Ashlyn."

"The worst of the storm is supposed to pass over us tonight. So you'll be here if there are any problems." He shook his head. "We've dealt with a lot of snowstorms, Mia. It's going to be fine. And if it's not, you know where to find me."

"I know," Mia said, her voice unnaturally high. Marco and his wife, Rosie, lived in a house just down the street and together they ran the behind the scenes functions of the hotel. Rosie cooked, and Marco covered everything else. "I just want to make sure I know what to do in a worst-case scenario."

And internally panic about everything going horribly and Janice deciding that Mia was unfit for the position of manager. But of course, she wasn't about to admit that to anyone but herself.

Her hip buzzed, and she pulled her phone out, reading the text from Ashlyn.

Jennifer is here.

"I've got to run. Thanks, Marco!"

She heard the barking before she left the stairwell. When Mia made it to the lobby, she knelt down on one knee and put her arms out for the rambunctious pug. Jennifer let go of the dog's leash, and he raced across the polished wood-planked floor and leapt into Mia's arms. Hugging him to her chest, she craned her neck to avoid Pug's slobbering as he showed her just how glad he was to be reunited.

"Thanks, Jen," Mia called as the teenager carried in a reusable grocery bag full of Pug's things. "How bad is it out there?"

Jennifer lifted one shoulder in a stereotypically teenage manner. "It's snowing."

Which Mia could see from looking out the window. "Thanks for watching him today."

"No problem. Just Venmo me."

"Right," Mia said. "I'll get right on that. Be safe out there."

She turned her attention back to Pug, rubbing his forehead with affection.

"A dog! Mommy, they have a dog!" A little girl ran into the lobby, her wet boots making muddy footprints across the wooden floor. "Can I pet it?"

"Sure," Mia said, holding Pug's little body as she searched behind the little girl for a mom, but no one was there. "Just let him smell your hand first."

The little girl had two long, brown ponytails and red ribbons tied to each one. She put one pudgy little hand forward and held it still while Pug sniffed at it and then proceeded to lick her fingers.

"What's your name?" Mia asked.

"Taylor," the girl said through giggles. "And my brother is Boston."

Mia glanced at the door again but there was no brother to be seen. Or parents, for that matter. Something about this girl tugged at Mia's memory and she felt like she knew her from somewhere.

A woman came through the front doors with long, black boots and highlighted hair curled back away from her face, searching the lobby with frantic eyes. "*Taylor*," she said sternly. "I asked you to wait in the car."

"But it was so cold outside," Taylor whined.

It was Elliot's sister, Amy. Mia grounded herself, preparing for a slew of questions, and said, "Hi, Amy. Welcome to Powder Peaks."

Amy seemed to notice her then for the first time. Her eyes narrowed as she scanned her memory and finally lit with understanding. "Mia," she said simply. "Wow, it's been so long."

Mia came to a stand, holding Pug under one arm to keep him still.

Amy crossed the lobby, taking her daughter by the hand. "You work here? What a coincidence."

"Yeah, really. I can get you checked in and show you up to your rooms if you're ready."

Her face wrinkled apologetically. "Oh, actually…I mean, this has nothing to do with *you* or anything, but I think we might try to get back home tonight."

Mia didn't know if there was any wisdom behind that plan. Amy and her family lived in the same small town Mia had grown up in—she got updates on the family from her mom whether she wanted to hear them or not—and their house was a good hour and a half away, at least. Longer in this weather.

"Do you know if Ell—" Amy cleared her throat. "If my brother has arrived?"

"Yes," Mia said, doing her best to look and sound professional. "Elliot checked into his room and left a while ago to grab dinner at Hal's."

"Perfect." She gave Mia a pitiful smile. "I better go track him down. It was good to see you," Amy said, dragging her daughter away.

Mia tried not to read too much into the farewell or how it sounded like Amy didn't expect to see her again.

Once the door shut behind them, she turned to Ashlyn. "Find the current weather report, please. I need to know if Parley's Canyon is open."

"Right away."

CHAPTER THREE

E lliot sat at the bar of the small restaurant, the remnants of his meal congealing on the plate in front of him. His phone buzzed repeatedly with texts from his agent.

You will agree to the commercial, right? It's easy money, man.

Elliot scanned the next eight texts that all said variations of the same thing. Frank was on his case every few days with a new opportunity he *simply couldn't pass up*. Elliot had specifically told Frank not to bother him for the week. His phone buzzed again, and he opened the text message.

It was a photo from his mom of his dad wearing a Santa kitchen apron and reindeer antlers. His parents were goofy, and he missed them. He'd spent long enough away, and he was ready for a change from the fast paced LA lifestyle and the constant need to be *on*. On for the cameras, for the fans, for social media and ad endorsements. The requirements of his job were around the clock, and it wore on him.

Of course, no one knew of these budding plans to leave LA but him. And the chances of the producers letting him out of his contract were slim.

He opened the message thread to Frank and typed.

I'm not talking business until after Christmas. I'll see you in a week.

Elliot felt his phone buzz as he slid it back into his pocket, but he ignored it. Frank could wait.

"Elliot!" a familiar voice said behind him, causing him to turn on his stool. His sister, Amy, was crossing the restaurant with a harried expression, dragging his niece by the arm. "Let's get out of here. I think if we hurry, we can probably make it home before the storm."

Home. Amy lived a few blocks from his parents. He could go *home* for Christmas. They hadn't done that in quite a few years. Not that he was complaining about Powder Peaks—as long as he was with his family, he was happy. But the idea of being home for Christmas squeezed his chest in a way he didn't want to closely identify.

"Hate to break it to you, babe," the bartender said, eyeing Amy, "But Parley's Canyon is closed. Just saw it on the news."

She cast the bartender a perfunctory glance before settling her determination back on her brother. "Then we'll go through Heber."

The bartender clicked his tongue. "Can't go that way either, sweetheart. It's a total white-out out there. Hope you've got a hotel, because like it or not, you're staying in Hidden Hollow tonight."

Amy looked between the bartender and her brother. Elliot watched with minor amusement as her gaze settled on him—it was better than giving in to the disappointment.

"Where's Brandon?" Elliot asked.

"In the car with Boston. He's not feeling well."

"Boston?"

"No," she corrected, "Brandon is not feeling well. He started getting nauseous on our way out of Salt Lake. I'm hoping he hasn't caught the flu that's been traveling around."

"My dad's gonna throw up," Taylor announced in her perfectly seven-year-old candidness.

Elliot got down from his barstool and swept his niece up into his arms. "Maybe we shouldn't announce that in a restaurant where people are eating, huh?"

"Okay, Uncle Elliot," she said. "But it's true."

"I'm sure it is." He set her down and tousled her hair. Pulling out his wallet, he flipped through his cash, selecting enough to cover his meal and the tip. He tossed it on the counter and took Taylor's hand, walking toward the door, Amy falling in behind him.

Amy's gaze was so strong while they walked down Main Street that Elliot could feel it. He hazarded a glance at her. "What?"

"I ran into someone at the hotel you might know."

Ah. So she'd seen Mia. Elliot was still trying to wrap his brain around having his ex-girlfriend run the hotel he was staying in. But he'd gone over the issue and determined the best course of action was to just leave her be. Regardless of how much he'd like to talk to her, she clearly still hated him, and he didn't want to make things worse. He would stay in his room or steer clear of the hotel completely. And she would likely give him the same wide berth she had in his hotel room.

"She looks really good," Amy said.

Yeah, she did. "What are you getting at here?"

"I just wondered how you felt seeing her again. It's been a while, hasn't it?"

A while? Try six years. Elliot refused to answer. His sister was just being nosy.

Amy sighed. "But I guess she's no Sophy Grant."

Elliot paused on the sidewalk. He tried to cast a stern look at Amy, but he didn't know if she was buying it. Her innocent blue eyes blinked back at him like she had no idea why he was bothered.

Snow landed on his face like cold pin pricks. Now was not the time or the location to hash out his love life. "So where'd you park?"

Amy rolled her eyes. "Just up here."

Their breath clouded before them as the cold permeated their layers. Snow fell in quick, fat flakes and gathered along their shoulders and the top of Amy's head, from what he could see.

They stepped up to the black Expedition parked on the road and Amy flipped the passenger door open to reveal Brandon laying back in the seat with the heater running full blast.

"The roads are closed," Brandon said, his voice groggy. "I've been listening to the radio. There's a massive wreck on the eighty and everything's shut down."

Brandon was lying back on the seat with his face hidden from view, his voice disembodied. Elliot released Taylor's hand and peeked inside the car to find Boston in the backseat, his eyes glued to the DVD player.

"Have you checked in yet?" Brandon asked, his eyes squeezed shut.

Amy sighed. "I'll go do that right now."

Mia knelt down and pushed Pug's bed further under the front desk. Ashlyn had just gone home for the day, and Mia was left to run the front desk and the other major hotel operations by herself until the next shift began at seven in the morning.

"Hello?" a voice rang out in the lobby. "Anyone here?"

Mia placed Pug on the bed and gave him a reprimanding finger, hoping he'd be obedient and stay put. She hopped up, giving Amy a bright smile. "Right here. Ready to check in?"

Amy nodded, tucking her hair behind her ear as she plopped her purse on the counter. "My husband is pretty sick, so I'd like to get him upstairs as soon as possible."

Mia sat at the computer chair and pulled up their reservation. "Your family has four suites reserved next to a single room. You've got the entire third floor. Would you like to be next door to Elliot's room or further down the hall?"

"Next door would be fine," Amy said.

Nodding, Mia began filling in information and sending documents to print for Amy's signature.

"So, Hidden Hollow, huh? I didn't know anyone else even knew about this tiny town," Amy said, leaning forward on the counter. "And driving up here was no joke."

"Yeah, the road up the mountain is a little windy. Probably not the best combination with a sick husband." Mia placed the printed pages before Amy on the counter. "If you could sign here, and initial there."

Amy scribbled on the pages before handing them back. "That's an understatement. I think I'll get my family up to the room and then sleep for a week."

The front doors opened and wind and snow trailed into the lobby behind the Kirkpatrick family.

"Here are your keys. It's room number 302, and the elevator is just down that hall." Mia pointed toward the narrow hallway to the left of the desk and waited for Amy to take the keys from the counter. "WiFi login information is in your room, the password is your last name and room number. Let me know if you need anything else."

Amy shot her a grateful smile.

Once she'd turned for the door again, Mia faced the Kirkpatricks. "How was the powder today?"

Their younger teenage son grinned at her, his cheeks still red from the cold and the wind. "Epic."

"The slopes were fantastic," Mr. Kirkpatrick agreed, slapping his son on the back.

"And the lodge was so warm and cozy," Mrs. Kirkpatrick added, her squat, round build opposing her husband's tall, wiry form. "I even finished my book."

"Be sure to check the lending shelves in the parlor if you need any more reading material," Mia said brightly.

Mrs. Kirkpatrick's eyebrows rose in delight. "I believe I shall. Erin?" She turned toward her teenage daughter, who didn't look as though she'd spent any time outside but rather sat in the lodge on her phone. Her face was glowing an eerie white color from staring into her phone now, which caused Mia to glance to the windows and notice how quickly the night had come. It was pitch dark outside.

"I'm good," Erin said, not taking her eyes from her screen.

"Well," Mrs. Kirkpatrick said brightly, "I can always look tomorrow. Goodnight, Mia."

"Goodnight, Mrs. Kirkpatrick. Feel free to call down to the front desk if you find yourself in need of anything."

They crossed the foyer and loaded into the elevator just as Elliot and his sister's family came through the front doors.

Amy wasn't kidding. Her husband looked horrible. He was tall with a dark beard and messy hair, his skin pale and drawn.

Elliot shot her a glance before hastily looking away. He carried his nephew while his sister led her daughter by the hand and her husband stalked behind them.

Mia should have called out some sort of greeting or offer of assistance like she would if it was any other family, but her tongue was stuck to the roof of her mouth. Elliot's short gaze had glued her to the spot. She was doing her utmost to push down the anger and hurt that flooded her afresh each time she saw him. Despair pricked at her body until she physically turned away from them, trying to catch her breath.

Old, buried betrayal and anger rose to her throat, threatening to claw its way into her heart. She coughed, startling when Pug nudged her leg with his wet nose. A small laugh escaped her throat and she bent down to pick him up, backing up until she was half sitting on the front desk, her back to the lobby.

"It's you and me, boy," she whispered. "We are going to watch Christmas movies all night long."

"Are the rest of the hotel guests invited to this party?"

Mia spun around to face the guest waiting at the desk. Elliot.

"Can I help you with something?" she asked, her voice tight.

He regarded her closely before clearing his throat. "Amy just wanted me to ask if you've got extra trash cans. She wants to set them around the room in case...well, in case Brandon needs them."

Mia nodded and set Pug on the floor. She tried to walk with all of the confidence of a woman who was not reliving her biggest heartbreak just moments before, but she was extremely aware of each move she made, and equally aware of Elliot's gaze hot on the back of her neck.

She led him to a closet at the end of the hallway across from the elevator, and unlocked it. "Trash cans?" she confirmed.

He nodded, and she selected a stack of garbage cans and handed a couple of them to Elliot.

Locating the garbage bags, Mia grabbed a roll and dropped it inside the buckets Elliot held. She caught his gaze. "Just in case."

"Thanks. This is great." He looked as though he wanted to say something more, and Mia warred with herself over whether or not she wanted to hear it. Six years was a long time, and so much had happened since the last time she saw him. But standing across from him now, close enough that she could reach forward and touch him, brought the old hurt back. She slammed the wall down again around her heart, scolding her own momentary weakness.

The lies, excuses, or whatever he had to say to explain his behavior would never make up for what he had done to her.

But part of her still wanted to hear it, all the same.

CHAPTER FOUR

E lliot stood in the narrow hallway beside the elevator and watched emotions shift like waves across Mia's face. He felt the desire to reach forward and brush a loose lock of blonde hair behind her ear but forced his hand to stay on the trash cans he held in his arms. If he had a hope of making any progress with her—not that he had *any* expectations—he needed to tread carefully.

"Listen, Mia," he began. "I just want to say—"

Ding!

The elevator sounded just before the doors slid open, and Elliot stepped to the side so whoever was inside would have room to pass him. He trained his gaze back on Mia as she looked at him with uncertainty—and a touch of curiosity, he believed. Or perhaps that was wishful thinking.

"You've *got* to be kidding me," a high-pitched voice said just beside him. "Elliot James. *The* Elliot James is standing in my hotel?"

He turned to find a teenaged girl grinning at him, her baggy Dodgers sweatshirt hanging halfway down her thighs.

"Erin," Mia said with an authority that impressed him. "Mr.

James is a guest at the Powder Peaks Lodge and as the Acting Manager I have to ask you to respect both his privacy and his space."

Erin shot Mia a quick glance before pulling out her phone. "Can I get a selfie?"

Elliot gave the teenager the wide smile he was used to directing at his female cast members. He wanted to get back to his conversation with Mia, and the sooner this girl was dealt with, the faster she would leave them alone. "Sure thing. Want me to take it?"

"Yes," Erin said, nearly throwing herself into his arms. He set down the trash cans. Careful not to drop her phone, he lifted it and framed himself and the girl in the photo. He could see Mia through the camera just behind him as she turned and locked the closet and then walked back toward reception.

Her face was pinched in disapproval, but was it because he'd accepted the selfie? Or was that just the way she was going to act around him for the duration of his stay?

He swallowed his frustration with himself. He'd only been trying to get the girl to leave them alone, and somehow he'd bungled it.

After taking the photo and handing the girl her phone, Elliot picked up the trash cans and pressed the elevator button to return to his sister's room.

"Thank you," Erin said, swiping through the pictures he took with a wide grin on her face. She lifted her gaze. "I just *love* you on *My Crazy Family*. That has to be my all-time favorite show right now."

"Thanks." He cast a glance around for Mia before stepping inside the elevator. He didn't see her anywhere. "See you around."

Erin stared at him like she hadn't thought of that herself. "I will. I *will* see you around."

Elliot had to remind himself that the teen was just excited, regardless of how insane she sounded.

Leaning forward, he pressed the button to close the doors, hoping Erin wouldn't get it in her mind to follow him and discover which room was his.

Once the doors were safely closed, he leaned against the wall and shut his eyes, clutching the garbage cans to his chest. That could have gone significantly better. He wasn't under the false illusion that he could get Mia to forgive him. But he *did* hope to find the opportunity to apologize, regardless. He couldn't see her face without remorse flooding him.

He was a guest at Powder Peaks for the next few days, at least. He had time.

The silence woke him up. Elliot turned toward the nightstand, but the clock was off, too.

The power had gone out.

He blew out a breath, stretching his arms high over his head and yawning. He'd grown used to the bustle of the city. The silence here was heavy and the darkness complete. He was positive he would not be going back to sleep anytime soon.

A deep, rumbling sound went off in the distance, and the red blinking light of the clock on the bedside table broke through the darkness.

Elliot lay in bed another few minutes before pulling himself up and padding across the floor to peek out the window. Peeling back the blackout curtains he was immediately flooded with a glowing light.

The moon and stars reflected off the snow, highlighting the

white blanket which covered Main Street and the surrounding mountains. And there was *a lot* of snow.

Elliot let the curtain swing back. He was dressed in a few short minutes and leaving his room before he could talk himself out of it. He paused at his sister's door and listened for the sound of disturbed children or a sick dad, but it was silent. Hopefully that meant the whole family was getting much needed sleep.

Pausing at the elevators, Elliot's hand hovered over the button before he thought better of it. If the power went back out, he would be stuck. Probably better to take the stairs.

The dim stairway was lit by small track lights lining the floor and he jogged down to the main level quickly. He didn't know exactly what he was going to say when he reached the lobby, but he felt the pull to go down there and check on Mia, regardless.

Eliott paused at the door and gathered a breath laced with courage, before stepping onto the main floor. Dark silence met him.

There were dim lights behind the front desk, but their light didn't reach very far. They were useful to highlight the empty desk, however. Elliot looked around briefly, but it didn't take long to confirm that Mia was missing. Well, it was worth a shot, but perhaps it would be better if he just went back to bed.

He turned for the stairwell again when a sudden, loud snore ripped through the foyer. Pausing, Elliot moved toward the parlor on the other side of the lobby. Two French doors sat open toward the foyer and he made his way across the wooden floor toward the room.

Peeking inside, Elliot could see Mia lying across the couch, a pug snuggled against her torso on the sofa cushion. Her mouth was open, and another snore tore through the room, putting a grin on his face.

Mia's shoulder-length blonde hair was tousled and her face peaceful. He had once loved her a lot, and those feelings didn't just dissipate over the years. It was painful to watch her now and know she was so angry with him, but he understood. He had left her without an explanation or a word. He'd ghosted her.

Now, six years later, it was well within her rights to despise him.

Which was why he was taking advantage of the opportunity to gaze at her without watchful, guarded eyes gazing back. He could probably never adequately apologize for what he'd put her through, and the regret which filled him as he watched her was acute.

She began to stir and he felt a moment's panic. What would Mia think to wake up and find Elliot standing over her, staring at her like a fool?

He was out of time. Her eyes blinked open, and Elliot stood rooted to the spot. He stared at her, sure she was going to be angry with him.

Instead, she surprised him by smiling softly, and his heart leapt to his throat.

"Elliot?" she questioned, her voice groggy from sleep.

"Yes." He tensed every muscle in his body, afraid to move and wreck the peace. His feet were glued in place, standing behind the sofa as Mia slowly woke up. Her arms stretched high above her head but immediately went down to her waist to check on the dog snoozing there. "Is everything all right?"

Elliot cleared his throat. "The power went out and woke me up, but it kicked back on."

Her eyebrows drew together. "Like sixty seconds later?"

"I guess so. I don't actually know."

"I bet that was the backup generators." Mia placed her hands around the dog and gently held him in place on the cushion as she got up from the couch. She looked to the TV. "I guess that explains why the TV is off."

Mia stepped past Elliot and crossed the lobby. He stared after her for a moment before following. She was treating him normally, and he didn't want it to end.

But he also recognized that she had just woken up, and he probably shouldn't push his luck.

She paused behind the desk and then glanced up to him. "Is there anything I can do for you?"

"Oh, no. I'm fine. I just have a hard time falling back asleep once I wake up, so I thought I'd come down here and make sure everything was all right."

Her pale eyebrows drew together slightly, but she nodded and went back to looking at something on her computer. A minute passed between them in silence and Elliot chose to take advantage of Mia's friendliness.

He leaned forward on the desk. "So how long have you been in Hidden Hollow?"

"About eight months."

She answered so easily. Distracted, maybe, but she answered. "And have you been in the hotel business for a while? Last I heard you wanted to become a lawyer."

"Ever since college," she said. Her face glowed from the computer screen. "I got a job at a front desk downtown and realized I loved the whole atmosphere and work involved in hospitality. I changed my major and pursued this instead."

"If I can be so bold, I'd have to say that this suits you far better than being a corporate lawyer. No matter how nice their suits are." He smiled, recalling a conversation once when Mia had confessed that part of the reason she wanted to be a lawyer was so she could wear power suits to big meetings.

"Well lucky for me this job requires suits every so often, too."

"Mia."

She stilled at the computer, bringing her gaze up to meet his. He could see the uncertainty in her blue eyes, and he hoped she would leave her guard down and allow him to speak.

He needed to apologize.

"Listen," he said, "I know we left things badly—"

"We?" she asked, her eyebrows shooting high on her forehead.

"No." Elliot shook his head. "Not we. *I* left things badly. I was a stupid, young kid and I was hurting—"

"I really don't know if I can do this right now." Her voice grew hard, and she waved her hand in dismissal, dropping her gaze.

"Please just let me say this, Mia. Then I promise to leave you be."

CHAPTER FIVE

M ia felt her heart beating a hundred miles an hour. Her whole body hummed with the proximity of the love of her life and his seemingly heartfelt apology. But what was the point?

She could never trust him again.

"I don't see how it's useful to keep rehashing the past," she said.

Elliot pierced her with a look so strong she wanted to glance away. But she held his gaze.

"I don't think we've rehashed the past at all," he argued.

"You know what I mean. You keep trying to bring it up."

"Which is not technically rehashing anything. I wouldn't mind talking about it though, for the record. I know I owe you an explanation. I'm willing to give you one."

Was it obvious that her heart stopped? For six years she'd wanted that very same thing. But no matter how many guys she dated or how many stupid episodes of *My Crazy Family* she'd watched, she could never shove that final conversation from her mind. The one that occurred in the hospital room following Elliot's accident.

Mia shook her head. "There's no point."

"Sure there is. Closure," he argued.

And Mia conceded, internally, that he did have a point. But stubbornness won out, and she looked back to her email. She lowered herself into the chair and opened the latest email from Janice, typing out a message about how things went the first day.

"Give me five minutes," Elliot said, his voice low. "Then I'll leave you alone."

Mia glanced at the time on the computer. Just past three o'clock in the morning. The poor man should go back to sleep so *she* could go back to sleep.

"Fine," she said, minimizing the email tab and turning her attention on Elliot. It was unfair how handsome he looked at three in the morning with a scruffy jaw and messy hair. Mia was positive she looked like a hot mess after waking up from a nap on the couch. She bit back the temptation to smooth her hair. "Five minutes."

"I know I handled things wrong. I have no excuses for my behavior except that I was a dumb kid, and I didn't know what else to do. When I got in the accident and lost my chance to go to the Olympics, I just sort of..." Elliot searched the dim room as though it held the answers. "I lost it."

"And couldn't answer the phone? Or texts? Or allow me into your room?"

Elliot cringed. "I *know* I was stupid."

"You proposed to me, Elliot," Mia said, her voice like steel. "You let me believe you would marry me. You told me you would heal and move on and prepare for the next Olympics and we could build a life together. Then the next thing I knew your mom told me you were gone and then your face was all over TV."

"I was only supposed to be a symbol. Like a motivational speaker," Elliot defended. "They liked my miracle story, and I was only supposed to be in a few commercials. But then the network picked me up and the rest just sort of happened."

"Sophy Grant just sort of happened?" Mia asked. She could hear the ice in her tone, and she closed her eyes, giving her head a small shake. "Forget it, Elliot. I thought I could be mature and listen to your side of the story and find a way to move forward with my life, but it just won't work." She lifted her gaze. "I think you should go back to your room."

Elliot peered at her, his mouth opening as though he wanted to argue. She continued to stare at him with determination until he closed his mouth again.

"Fine." Elliot stalked back toward the stairwell. The door shut behind him with a thud, resounding off the walls.

Mia felt empty.

Had she overreacted? No. It was within her rights to be angry. The man had promised her the world, then dropped her without a single word. In fact, she was fairly sure the last time she'd heard from him was when he was promising to buy a ring and get down on one knee after his back healed.

He'd told her the accident was an epiphany. That it'd showed him the only thing that mattered in his life was *her*. And the worst part of it all was that she had believed him.

The morning sun peeked over the horizon and sent shafts of light through the parlor windows. Mia forced herself up and gently scooted around Pug to get off of the couch. Guests could be awaking any moment and she needed to make sure they would be able to get out the front door.

Obtaining her coat, hat, and gloves, she forced the front door open just enough to slip through with a shovel.

The roads hadn't been plowed yet, but it was still early. Snow came up to Mia's knees, immediately soaking through her pants as she got to work shoveling away the snow from the hotel entrance.

She got the snow cleared just before the door by the time Hannah showed up for her shift.

"You know Marco usually does that, right?" Hannah said, arching an annoying eyebrow.

Mia slicked away the sweat from her forehead with the back of her wrist. "Well good thing I didn't wait for him or you wouldn't be able to get in."

Hannah shot her a small smile before opening the door and going inside. Mia heard boots stomping against the rug just inside the door. If Hannah was here, then it was nearly seven in the morning. She needed to make sure the kitchen was open.

It's not like she could expect the guests to all trample out into the snow. It was difficult to walk in when it was this deep. And if no one plowed the mountain roads then the people who didn't live in town would have no way to get to their restaurants to open them.

If Mrs. Bruin brought her tiny terrier out here, the poor thing would be swallowed in snow immediately.

Mia leaned her shovel against the side of the building and went back inside. The smell of breakfast cooking wafted through the foyer and forced her stomach to growl. Phew. Rosie must have slipped in the back door.

"Smells like breakfast is ready," a cheerful voice said to her right. She turned to find Mrs. Kirkpatrick and her son sitting in the overstuffed chairs beside the fireplace, facing the tree.

"Good morning, Kirkpatrick family. I hope you had a restful night."

"You are really wet," the boy said, eyeing her up and down.

Mia smiled at him brightly, overcompensating for her exhaustion. "Yes, I am. Thanks to the snow out there." She tried to sound cheerful but she could tell she was flagging. She'd stayed up until two in the morning watching Christmas romantic comedies, and she hadn't managed to fall back asleep after her visit with Elliot.

Needless to say, she was in need of a nap. And some dry pants.

The clock rang out from the parlor indicating the turn of the hour. Clapping her hands together, Mia said, "Kitchen's open."

Mrs. Kirkpatrick rose, her son following her toward the hallway beside the parlor.

Once the guests cleared the lobby, Mia crossed to the front desk, peeling off her gloves as she went. "I'm off the clock," she said, gathering Hannah's attention. "But I'll just be in room 202 if you need anything."

"The room with the broken sink?" Hannah asked, her scrunched up nose proving her disgust.

"It's not that bad. But yeah, I'm just staying in there while Janice is gone this week so I'm close if you need anything." And due to the snow, she didn't know how long it would take her to get home anyway. It was a really good thing she brought extra dog food just in case.

Hannah popped her gum. "Okay."

"And one more thing," Mia said, coming closer to the desk and lowering her voice. "We've got a VIP guest this week, and he's already been bothered by the other guests for selfies. I promised him we would do our best to keep the fans away so he could enjoy his stay in relative peace."

Hannah perked up at once. "Who is it?"

Mia ground her back teeth, calling on her inner strength. "Hannah, do you understand what I'm asking of you?"

Hannah looked impatient. "Yes, of course. Don't let the average guests overrun the VIP guest. Now tell me, who is it?"

"Elliot James."

"Shut up," Hannah said, her eyes growing wide.

Mia reared back in shock, until she realized that Hannah was just excited. "As a member of staff, Hannah, you need to be part of the team that *protects* our VIP guest, not someone who drools over him and takes discreet photos for Instagram."

She scoffed. "I would never do that. I value my job too much."

Well, that was a relief. Mia tapped the counter. "I value my sleep. I'll check back in a couple hours. But please come wake me up if there are any emergencies or anything I should be made aware of. Under no circumstances should you contact Janice."

"Gotcha. Boss."

Mia turned away, ignoring the acid Hannah slipped into those words. Hannah had been up for Assistant Manager originally when Mia was brought in from another company, and Mia knew the girl never forgave her for stealing her job. Or, at least that was probably how Hannah saw things.

Mia knew she was more qualified for the position.

Retrieving Pug from the parlor where the lazy dog still slept on the sofa, Mia went upstairs and let herself into the room with the broken sink. It wasn't the end of the world. The small sink in the kitchenette still worked fine. But it made the room unusable for guests until Marco had a chance to fix it.

And it made the room available to her for the week.

She turned on the shower and situated Pug on the bed before peeling off her wet clothes and hopping into the water. The hot, steamy water felt so good; if she wasn't careful, she'd fall asleep right there.

Instead, she ran her late-night conversation with Elliott through her mind over and over again. The guy had a point. It would do them both some good to get closure. The only problem was that Mia became infused with anger every time she saw his face.

And she wasn't feeling ready to let it go.

CHAPTER SIX

E lliot had never been so stressed trying to eat breakfast in his entire life. He regretted ever asking Amy if he could take Taylor and Boston downstairs to eat, but he'd only been trying to help out.

And now there was chaos everywhere.

Erin, the teenager from last night, was filming everything he did, and her parents were doing nothing to stop it—or they were oblivious.

The boy who appeared to be her brother was whining that he was bored and wanted to snowboard.

There was a woman crying loudly with a small dog on her lap because she was so worried she wouldn't make it home in time for Christmas with all of the snow.

And to top it all off, Elliot's own niece and nephew were making a huge mess with their scrambled eggs.

Elliot was ready to climb back up to his room and shut the world away. But he couldn't just leave the kids. Or the mess.

Where was Mia, anyway?

He leaned forward. "Hey Boston, are you finished eating?"

His nephew looked up at him through wide brown eyes. "Yeah."

"Awesome." Elliot stood, waiting for the kids to follow him. "You guys want to go see the Christmas tree?"

"Yes!" they answered in unison.

Score.

Elliot led the children down the hall.

He'd checked in with the front desk when he woke up and assured himself the power was back on and they weren't relying on the generator anymore.

A brunette at the front desk gave him a double take when he approached and he shot her his winning smile. It was likely going to aid him in getting what he wanted, even though he knew it was probably against hotel policy—Mia's number.

"Elliot James," the front desk attendant said with a saucy smile. She pulled her long, dark hair over her shoulder and leaned forward on her elbows. "What can I do for you?"

He glanced to her name tag. "Well, Hannah, there's a lot of chaos in the dining room right now, and I figured your manager should probably be made aware."

Hannah's evident pleasure at being addressed by her first name was immediately overcast with irritation. "Our *assistant* manager is not in at the moment. What is the nature of the chaos?"

"Upset guests and rambunctious children, mostly."

Hannah glanced behind him toward the elevator and then down to her phone.

"I don't mind calling and complaining to the manager, if that makes it easier for you," Elliot said. "If you could just give me her number…"

"I'm sorry, we can't reveal that sort of information to a guest."

Darn. Elliot glanced over his shoulder to his niece and nephew and found them both examining the ornaments on the tree. "You could dial the number and hand me the phone?" Elliot asked.

"I'm sorry, I don't think that would be appropriate."

Elliot tried to swallow his frustration. "What time does she get back in?"

"She'll be down whenever she wakes up. I was under strict orders not to bother her while she takes a nap."

So she was still in the hotel. Excitement bubbled up in Elliot's chest. "And what room number is she staying in?"

"Two-oh—" Hannah blinked, stopping herself. "How did you know she was in the hotel?"

"Just a guess. You were saying?"

Hannah gave him a knowing smile. "I can't reveal that information."

Elliot chuckled. He shook his head. He was so close to discovering where to find Mia. Turning away from the front desk, he approached his niece and nephew. "You guys finding some cool ornaments?"

"Yes!" Boston said, grinning. The kid was missing three teeth, which made for a wonky smile. But it was cute all the same.

"Great. Let's head up and check on your dad."

He got Boston and Taylor to the stairwell and up to level two. Before Hannah the receptionist caught herself, she had said *two-oh*. That meant that Mia was sleeping in one of these rooms.

Crouching low, Elliot drew his niece and nephew closer. "Do you guys want to play a game?"

They both nodded their heads eagerly. Good.

"This is how we play. You guys run down this hallway and knock on all of the doors. Loudly."

"And what happens?" Taylor asked, tilting her head to the side.

"The hotel lady will come out of one of these doors, and if you're the one who knocked on her door, you get a dollar."

Both of their faces brightened at the prospect of money. "Can we get something from the vending machine in the stairs?"

"Sure thing," Elliot said. His niece and nephew turned for the hall and immediately started banging on each of the doors down the hallway which, incidentally, all began with *two-oh*.

But the racket these kids were making was *loud*. A lot louder than Elliot expected. He rose to his full height and started opening the door to the stairwell again. Maybe it was better to hide behind the door and pretend he didn't know what had gotten into Taylor and Boston.

A door opened midway down the hall and an older woman poked her head out of her room. He recognized her as the woman from the breakfast room who had the terrier, crying about making it home in time for Christmas.

She looked down the hall at the kids banging on doors and Elliot realized just how reckless this plan was. He pushed open the door all the way and stepped into the hallway. What had gotten into him? Had he really wanted to see Mia *so badly* that he sent his niece and nephew down a hall of rooms banging on doors to wake her up? Probably from a much-needed nap, too.

And all with the flimsy excuse of something that another worker had probably already handled.

"I am so sorry," Elliot said, approaching the woman where she stood halfway down the hall. "Taylor, Boston, that's enough guys!"

The older woman shook her head. "Kids these days. No one knows how to tame them."

The door at the very end of the hall opened then, and Mia poked her head through the opening, her eyes blinking as though she'd just awoken and her hair disheveled. Man, she was beautiful.

It was difficult to regret his foolish actions when this was the result.

"What's going on?" she asked when her gaze landed on Elliot and the older woman.

"We found her!" Boston said, loudly. He ran back to Elliot. "We found her!"

"I can see that." He pulled out his wallet and handed Boston and Taylor each a dollar. "Why don't you guys head to that vending machine and pick a snack?"

Phew. That could have been much worse. They could have announced how Elliot had paid them to make the noise.

"Ms. Murphy," the older woman said. "Might I have a word? I tried to speak to your receptionist, but she wasn't very helpful."

Mia glanced between Elliot and the woman before looking down at her own sock-endowed feet and candy cane leggings. Elliot heard her sigh. She flipped the lock on her door and let it close so the lock would catch the door and stay open. Pulling her robe tighter, she padded down the hallway in her socks, giving the older woman a bright smile.

"What can I do for you, Mrs. Bruin?"

Mrs. Bruin's eyes welled up with tears. "I can't go home today, dear. The road out of town was damaged in the storm and no one can get through. I am stuck in Hidden Hollow, and it is nearly Christmas. I am unable to do all of the lovely things I am used to doing the week of Christmas. I cannot hand out cookies to my neighbors or carol with my church choir, and I certainly cannot sit by the light of the Christmas tree and watch my movies."

Mia looked calm, but the way her eyes flicked about caused Elliot to believe she was panicking internally. She focused on Mrs. Bruin. "I am so sorry to hear that. I am sure if you check in with the front desk, they will extend your room at no charge until the road becomes passable. And we can all hope the roads will clear well before Christmas."

Mrs. Bruin's head whipped up at once. "They didn't offer me that."

Mia smiled. "Leave it to me, Mrs. Bruin, and I'll take care of it. I'm sorry for the inconvenience and hope to make your stay at Powder Peaks Lodge a pleasurable one in spite of the circumstances."

Mrs. Bruin stepped forward and grasped Mia's wrist. "You have no idea what this means to me."

Mia looked back at the woman with equal intensity. "The pleasure is mine. Now, where did you hear about the damage to the road?"

"From Mr. Kirkpatrick," Mrs. Bruin said. She turned back for her room, scooping up her dog as she stepped inside. Her smile was wide and satisfied.

The door closed, leaving Mia and Elliot alone in the hallway. "That was really nice of you," he said. "She was pretty distraught this morning in the dining room."

Mia gave him a smile that didn't reach her eyes. "It's my job."

"Well, it's not your job," he countered. "You're not required to offer her a free room. That was above and beyond. And you should realize that your actions made her very happy."

Mia couldn't hold his gaze. Was she uncomfortable with the praise?

"Did you need something, too?" she asked, her blonde eyebrows lifting. "Do you know what she meant by damage to the road?"

"Actually, I don't. Sorry. I was hoping to speak with you at some point but clearly now is not the right time." He indicated her state of dress, and her cheeks colored as she pulled the robe tighter around herself.

"It's fine," she said over a yawn. "I'm up now anyway, and I've got to figure out what's going on with the road. What can I help you with?"

"It really doesn't matter now. The breakfast room was a mess this morning. I don't know what was going on, but it was just chaos."

Her eyebrows pulled together, and she crossed her arms over her chest. "Can you be more specific?"

Elliot indicated Mrs. Bruin's door with his thumb and then stepped closer to Mia, further from the older woman's door. "She was upset and loud about it. The teenagers were whining that they couldn't leave the hotel and were bored. And their parents weren't doing anything about it."

He left off Erin's constant filming of him. He could tell it had bothered Mia when Erin had asked for the selfie. Probably best not to bring up more social media fodder now.

"It sounds like everyone was a little stir crazy."

"Exactly," Elliot agreed, as his niece and nephew ran back into the hall.

"I got Goldfish!" Boston yelled, running toward them.

Taylor came at a much slower pace, but said equally as loud, "And I got M&Ms."

"Nice, guys."

"I wonder…" Mia paused, looking between Elliot and the children. "Hey, your family has the Wasatch Room booked all week for activities. Are you planning on utilizing it today?"

He shrugged. "Without my parents here, I doubt we'll do any of the activities they planned."

A genuine smile lit her lips and warmed Elliot's heart. When she looked at him that way, he wanted to give her the world. But use of the Wasatch Room would suffice for now.

"Would it be terribly unprofessional of me to ask if I can use that room today, then? You won't be charged for it."

"Of course you can use it," Elliot said right away. "What can I do to help?"

Mia began turning back toward her room and paused, looking over her shoulder. "You mean that?"

"Yes."

She looked thoughtful. "Meet me there in twenty minutes, and I'll put you to work."

"Deal," he said with a decisive nod, electricity pumping through his veins. Maybe it was the spirit of the holidays and a magical shift in the atmosphere forcing Mia to agree to spend time with him. Or, maybe it was her desperate need for help. He didn't care which, he was just glad she wasn't avoiding him completely.

He turned to the kids. "Come on, guys, let's go check on your dad."

He had no idea what Mia had in mind or what type of work she was going to make him do, and he didn't care. He got to spend time with her. If their past interactions were any indication, the more time they spent together, the more comfortable she became.

It would only be a matter of time before she was willing to allow him to explain and apologize.

CHAPTER SEVEN

Was she crazy? Mia pulled on her clothes and brushed out her hair before tying it back in a ponytail with a red scrunchy. It wasn't unusual for a hotel to put on activities. But usually they were planned in advance and marketed. *This* had the potential to flop.

Mia would just have to make sure it didn't flop. Nothing was going to ruin this week, and when she'd heard Elliot's report of the dining room at breakfast, she'd nearly flipped out. Internally, of course. She hoped Elliot couldn't tell how much it had bothered her.

Leaving her room, Mia closed the door softly behind her and took the stairs down to the dining room. She poked her head in, but it was empty and spotless. Thanks to the kitchen and cleaning staff, she was sure.

She approached the kitchen and found Rosie preparing vegetables on the cutting block.

"Rosie, do you know what's happening with the roads?"

"There was an avalanche last night and it broke the bridge that runs over Hansen Creek."

"What?" Mia said, shocked. "That's the only way out of town."

Rosie nodded, her focus on the carrots she was chopping. "Plows couldn't get past it, so the roads are all covered in snow."

Well, that certainly explained why they hadn't gone down Main Street by the time Mia had awoken. "What's the estimated time to fix it?"

Rosie shook her head. "Marco spoke with the Sheriff this morning, and they've called into Park City for some reinforcements. They think the snow should be cleared quickly, but they have to deal with their own town first. And then they need to fix the bridge."

"So who knows how long we'll be stuck here." Mia blew a breath out through her teeth. "Well, at least we have power. Do we have popcorn?"

The cook looked up, evidently surprised by the request. "Yes. There's a whole jug of kernels for the air popper."

"Perfect. Can you pop it and have it sent to the Wasatch Room? In maybe three or four of those large bowls?"

Rosie nodded. "Sure thing."

"And do we have any cranberries?"

Rosie squinted. "We do, but I was planning to use them on Christmas."

Hopefully there won't be anyone left on Christmas. "The roads should be cleared and fixed before then, right? If I use your cranberries now would it ruin everything?"

Rosie gave Mia an endearing smile. "It would ruin nothing. You can have them."

"Wonderful. You're the best, Rosie."

"I know," the cook called after Mia as she left the room.

Taking herself down the hall, Mia passed the Wasatch Room and inhaled a few calming breaths before approaching Hannah at the front desk.

She was proud of herself for not flinching when the brunette receptionist snapped her gum. "Hannah, I'm going to be holding Christmas activities in the Wasatch Room available to all guests. Will you call around to the occupied rooms and make sure they are aware, or should I do it myself really quickly?"

Hannah eyed her a moment before reaching for the phone. "I can handle this."

"Great." Mia gave her a bright smile. "Did you hear about the bridge?"

"Yes," Hannah said, popping her gum again. "My dad says they'll have it cleared up in a day or two."

Hopefully he was correct. Mia crossed the lobby and took the hallway near the parlor back toward the Wasatch Room.

She paused halfway down the hallway when she found Elliot waiting outside of the room, leaning against the wall with his hands in his pockets like a James Dean character from the fifties. Her heart fluttered. Why had she asked him to come help? It couldn't have been desperation because she clearly had everything under control.

It had to have been a moment of weakness. She needed to manage her heart better and let her brain control her actions when Elliot was around.

"Thanks for coming," she said, pulling out her keys to unlock the room. Elliot followed her inside and she pointed to a few long tables stacked against the wall. "Will you begin setting those up? Two or three ought to be enough."

Mia tried to ignore the way Elliot's long-sleeved t-shirt clung to his back when he lifted the entire table by himself as though it was no heavier than a bag of chips. But she'd kissed this guy before. Many, many times, in fact. And she knew just how it felt to be held in those arms.

Facing away from Elliot, Mia shook the memories before they could overwhelm her. She found the sound control panel and connected her phone. It took a moment to find the right volume, but once she did, she set the phone to shuffle her Christmas music album, and it set the mood perfectly.

"That's nice," Elliot said. He'd set up three tables and began adding chairs.

Mia passed him. "I'll be right back."

It took her no more than five minutes to go to the supply closet and locate a good handful of sewing kits. She returned to find the chairs completed and bowls of popcorn on two of the tables. *I Saw Mommy Kissing Santa Claus* played over the speakers and the buttery scent of popcorn reached her nose.

"Where are the cranberries?" she asked Elliot.

"Rosie said she had to go back for them. And another bowl of popcorn."

"First name basis already?" Mia teased, crossing the room to stand on the other side of the table from Elliot. Any space between them was good space—more room to think, to breathe, and to *not* pick up his familiar scent. She crossed her arms over her chest. "You get friendly with the staff pretty quickly."

His smile slipped momentarily. "It helps that everyone here wears a nametag."

"*Touché.*"

"Did I hear there are Christmas activities in this room?" Mrs. Bruin called as she stepped inside.

"Yes," Mia answered, placing sewing kits at each chair. "Welcome. Please choose a seat and we'll get started."

Mrs. Bruin crossed the room and pulled out the chair directly next to where Elliot was standing. Mia bit back a chuckle at the woman's eagerness and wondered if Mrs. Bruin had ever watched an episode of *My Crazy Family* or if she had merely taken a liking to the handsome guest.

When Elliot glanced up and caught Mia's eye, they shared a moment of silent humor when both of them lifted their eyebrows at the exact same time as though they were communicating: *this is interesting.*

The Kirkpatrick family joined them next, filing into the other side of the table and were shortly followed by Rosie with bowls of cranberries stacked on top of a third enormous bowl of popcorn. Mia took the bowls from the cook's arms. "Thank you, Rosie."

"It was nothing." Rosie turned to go.

Mia cleared her throat, placing the bowls of cranberries beside popcorn at each table. "We are going to be stringing garland today to decorate the lodge." She finished passing out the miniature sewing kits. "If you need help, I can assist with getting your needles started. And my only piece of advice is to be gentle with the popcorn. But otherwise, have at it."

Chatter grew louder among the patrons as they began to work. Amy showed up about ten minutes later with both of her children, and they claimed a table of their own. Mia sat across from Amy after she handed out sewing kits and offered to help the kids with their needles.

"That would be great," Amy said, untangling her string. "I don't think I've done a garland like this in years, Mia. What a great idea."

Taylor untangled her own thread, her eyebrows drawn together as she focused on the task. "What do we do with it when we're done, Mommy?"

"They can go on a Christmas tree or a mantle," Amy said.

"Or," Mia added, "you can hang it in the hotel room if you want to decorate your own space."

Taylor's face brightened. "Oh, can we, Mommy? I want one above my bed."

"I want one above my bed, too!" Boston added around a mouthful of popcorn.

Taylor shot her brother a sassy smirk. "You won't get one above your bed if you eat all the popcorn first."

"Be nice," Amy admonished.

"Unless I help Boston," Mia said. "What do you think,

buddy?"

"Yes, please," he answered around another fistful of popcorn. It was a good thing Rosie made so much or there wouldn't be enough for both the snacking and the garland.

Holiday music played in the background as the hotel guests chatted amiably and strung their garland. Amy was halfway through her length of thread when she paused and looked at Mia closely.

Mia's needle hesitated while poking a piece of popcorn, but Boston took over sliding the popcorn down the thread. "Do I have something on my face?"

"No." Amy shook her head. "I was just trying to remember when I saw you last. That's all."

Probably six years ago, Mia thought. Once Elliot completely dropped her, she'd turned around and dropped his whole family. It was something she regretted periodically over the years as she heard about weddings and births and wanted to catch up with people she had grown so close to while she'd dated Elliot. But at the time, it was easier for her to have a clean break. She had been part of Elliot's life for four years, and that was a long time to have invested in his family.

"I think Taylor was a baby when I saw you last," Mia said, attempting to be diplomatic.

"Yeah, I think you're right." Amy focused on the cranberry in her fingers, but her needle didn't move. "What a shame," she said quietly, and Mia wondered if she was supposed to have heard it or not.

Mia glanced around the other tables and the guests who were cheerfully stringing their garlands. She would have patted herself on the back for coming up with a successful activity in under twenty minutes, but that would draw weird looks, so she refrained.

By the time the garlands were finished, however, no one stood to leave the room. Mia and Taylor were the last to work on their threads, but Mia found, with interest, that the other table was comfortable and content, chatting and snacking on leftover popcorn—Mrs. Bruin more than most, the way her adoring gaze kept falling on Elliot.

Mia leaned forward. "I think your brother has an admirer."

Amy's eyebrows rose and she turned to look at the other table. Mrs. Bruin was gazing up at Elliot like a lovesick woman and Amy burst out in laughter, spitting popcorn pieces all over the table.

"Ew Mom!" Boston said, backing away from the wet popcorn pieces.

Amy kept laughing, and Mia chuckled as she got up to fetch something to wipe it up with.

When she returned from the supply closet with a roll of paper towels and a bottle of cleaning spray, she jumped again to find Elliot standing in the hallway precisely as he had when she'd come upon him earlier—James Dean style. Leaning back, hands in pockets.

She tried to pass him, but he put out a hand to halt her. "Can we talk?"

She lifted the paper towels and cleaning solution. "It's not a good time."

Elliot nodded, but his face was resigned. Her stomach dropped at his disappointment and the knowledge that she had caused those feelings. But why wasn't he getting the message? If she wanted to talk to him, she would have done so already.

"Maybe later?" he asked.

Mia paused before going back into the room. "Elliot, I tried to give you a chance last night to explain yourself and you didn't really say anything. It kind of feels pointless."

She pushed the door open and stepped inside. By the time she'd cleaned up the mess and announced that afternoon's activity, she'd glanced back to the door at least forty times.

And Elliot never came back inside.

CHAPTER EIGHT

"You could show Mia you still love her with a grand gesture," Amy said, lounging on the couch in her suite. Her kids were both glued to the television where the classic Grinch movie was playing, and Brandon was still out of commission in his room. Luckily their suite included a bedroom with a door so Brandon could rest in complete privacy.

"I didn't ask for advice," Elliot said, spearing his sister with a look. "And I don't still love Mia."

Her eyebrows lifted, but she didn't back down. "Then tell me more about Sophy Grant. You know, for having a famous brother I really get none of the perks."

"What perks are those?"

"Red carpet events. Premieres. Meeting famous people."

"I don't really do much of that," Elliot said. Which was true. He did the bare minimum when it came to publicity. "And I don't know how many times I have to say this, but those photos with Sophy were a one-time thing. The date went horribly, and we never pursued a relationship."

"Hey, I can dream, all right?"

"About Sophy Grant?" Elliot asked, arching an eyebrow.

"No," his sister said at once, "about my brother being cool enough to date someone famous."

Elliot chuckled. "Drop your expectations. I won't ever be that cool." And he didn't want to be. The expectations placed on his shoulders after he began dating Sophy were too much. And subsequently, the relationship hadn't lasted long.

Amy's gaze flitted across the room, landing on her children. "Mia said there was going to be a movie in the Wasatch Room at four. I guess there's a really nice projector and the hotel has a small collection of holiday films."

"Nice."

"Should we go?" Amy asked, carefully keeping her gaze on her children. She wasn't fooling him, though. He knew she was waiting impatiently for his answer.

Elliot executed a small shrug, his attention on the TV, just like the kids. He wondered if he was even fooling his sister. Of course he'd want to go. Any time he got to spend around Mia was equally hurtful and thrilling. He didn't quite know where he was going to land when the week was through, but after six years of silence from her, one thing was abundantly clear: he really, *really* missed having Mia in his life. And the dumbest part was that he hadn't even realized it until he was around her again.

He was such an idiot for letting her go. But he hadn't been in his right mind then.

"Let's just hang out here," Amy said, nestling into the couch more. "The kids are already watching a movie, and I'm satisfied."

"Sure," Elliot nodded, trying to figure out a way to slip out of the room without being obvious.

Amy surprised him a minute later by saying, "Did you hear about Adam's scholarship?"

"No," Elliot said. Their older brother, Jake, didn't usually call Elliot with updates about his family.

"He got a full ride to the University of Utah."

Elliot was suitably impressed. His eyebrows rose, and he tore his gaze away from the Grinch shoving a tree up a fireplace. "I didn't realize the kid was even in high school," he confessed.

Amy rolled her eyes. "Your nephew, you mean? He's a junior. He'll graduate early."

"Why didn't Jake put that in the family chat message?"

"Who knows," Amy said, burrowing further down on the couch. "Probably because he told most of us at a Sunday dinner."

Elliot tried to swallow his annoyance, but the more he considered it, the more irritated he grew. If he was living at home, he would know these sorts of things. He would be going to those bi-monthly family dinners. But he wasn't anywhere near Utah anymore. He lived in LA now. The least his family could do would be to inform him when important things were going on in their lives.

Standing, Elliot picked up his phone and shoved it in his pocket. "I need to go for a walk."

"Okay," Amy called, a suggestive smile on her lips. If only she realized he was leaving due to discomfort now, and not a desire to see Mia.

But still, his feet automatically carried him down the stairwell and around the lobby toward the Wasatch Room. The hallway was dark when he approached with white and blue lights spilling from the room and reflecting on the wall, indicating the movie had already begun.

It didn't surprise him in the least that the movie Mia chose to play was *Miracle on 34th Street*. She had always loved old movies. He'd given her a hard time in high school when he'd discovered the James Dean poster on her wall. But she was relentless in her abiding love for Audrey Hepburn, Fred Astaire, and Gene Kelly. She'd had a shelf full of black and white movies from "the golden era," as she'd put it.

Elliot peeked inside the room and found Mia sitting on one of two sofas. The furniture looked familiar and he was pretty sure it was from the parlor. Mrs. Bruin sat on the other end of Mia's sofa, and Mrs. Kirkpatrick had a seat on the other one beside her son. There was no obvious space for Elliot to sit, so he hovered in the doorway, determining whether he wanted to go in or not.

But Mia was in there, her head leaning on the back of the sofa. He stepped inside.

Everyone turned to look at him as he approached the couches. Mrs. Bruin immediately shooed the dogs from the cushion between herself and Mia. Elliot watched it happen with reserve and then looked to Mia, but her face gave nothing away. The movie had already begun, and he didn't want to cause a scene, however, so he just took the seat Mrs. Bruin patted suggestively and attempted to settle in.

"You missed the beginning," Mrs. Bruin said, leaning over, "but it shouldn't be too hard to catch yourself up."

"I've seen the movie before," he informed her with a smile, hoping his closed lips would portray to the older woman precisely how quiet they should be.

She got the hint and settled into the couch, returning her focus to the movie.

Elliot was ultra-aware of Mia's proximity. Her elbow brushed against his arm as she reached forward to pick up her dog and settle him on her lap, and Elliot drew a sharp breath. It was torture to be so near her and yet still feel so emotionally distant. Was this really that much better than sitting up in his hotel room waiting for the snow to stop coming down and the road to be fixed?

Elliot hazarded a glance at Mia, and her soft smile while she watched the movie, her hand stroking her pug's head, warmed his soul.

Yes. This really was much better.

Mia stroked Pug's head, doing her best to keep her attention on the movie. But it was difficult with Elliot sitting so casually beside her. She thoroughly enjoyed *Miracle on 34th Street*, but it seemed to drag now. By the time the movie came to a close, Mia put Pug on the floor and shot up before Elliot could waylay her with any conversation.

"Warning," she announced to the occupants of the room, "lights are going on."

She turned on the lights and moved to the projector to begin putting it away.

"Thank you, Ms. Murphy," Mrs. Kirkpatrick called as she led her son from the room. He followed his mom, blinking rapidly through a yawn. He had likely just woken up. Which made sense. Mia had wondered how the kid had sat through the whole movie without leaving.

The movie hadn't been as successful as the garland activity. Mia filed that bit of information away for future use.

"Have a good evening now," Mia said.

Busying herself with the projector and its case, Mia didn't notice when Elliot approached her. Gray leather shoes appeared out of the corner of her eye and she followed them up to his face.

"Mrs. Bruin asked me to inform you that she won't be needing her cake tonight," Elliot said with amusement. "She would have told you herself, but she needed to take her dog outside."

"She didn't call for it last night, either," Mia said absently. "I wonder if she's sick of it."

Elliot shrugged, his green eyes sparkling with amusement. "Need a hand?"

Mia should say no. She should ask him to leave. Any self-respecting woman would continue to push him away, right? She opened her mouth to ask him to give her space and said, "Sure. Want to put the projector in that case?"

That had been unintentional. She tried to ignore the warmth that filled her when he held her gaze, triumph in his green eyes.

Elliot moved to take the projector, and Mia crossed the room to put up the screen by a button near the sound panel. What had gotten into her? She should have pushed him away. Apparently she was a glutton for punishment, but it was easier than she'd expected to slip back into the familiarity they once held.

"Are you working through Christmas?" Elliot asked from across the room, his voice echoing slightly.

"Yeah. I'm covering for my boss while she's in Arizona visiting her family for the holidays."

Elliot nodded. He held her gaze for a moment before focusing back on the task at hand.

"And it's a lot more pressure than I expected."

He didn't respond right away, and Mia leaned against the wall, watching the screen rise slowly into the ceiling. She kept talking, though she didn't know why. It was just comfortable with Elliot. Even after all of the pain and heartache and years, being around him was easy—though she hated to admit it, even to herself. "It's not too much pressure, of course," she continued, "but being *assistant* manager is so easy because I can always pass on the difficult things to Janice."

"You've handled everything really well so far," Elliot said. "As far as I've seen."

Mia shot him a self-deprecating smile. "There hasn't really been anything terrible so far."

"Besides being snowed in and stuck in this tiny town surrounded by nothing but a broken road and mountains."

"Yeah, besides that," Mia agreed with a chuckle. "But it's been manageable." She reached over and tapped her knuckles on the wood paneling.

"Still superstitious?" Elliot asked with a grin.

Mia shook her head but smiled in a teasing manner. "Maybe. Do you still make a wish when the clock says eleven-eleven?"

Elliot closed the projector case and held her gaze. "I do."

"Has it ever worked? Making a wish on the clock?"

"Not yet," Elliot said, shaking his head. He started walking toward her. "But it will soon. I hope."

Mia leaned back against the wall, crossing her arms over her chest.

"Why do you always do that around me?" Elliot asked, coming to stand directly in front of her. His eyes were serious, set on her with purpose.

"What are you talking about?"

He pointed to her arms. "Every time we talk one-on-one, you cross your arms. What are you guarding yourself from?"

Mia dropped her arms to her sides. If she was protecting herself from Elliot, it was subconsciously done. Not that it wasn't necessary. "You."

Elliot arched one eyebrow, and Mia took the opportunity with him so close to examine his face. He hadn't shaved in a few days, and the scruff was attractive, making him look the rugged snowboarder he was when she'd dated him all throughout high school and their first year of college. Something about him looking more like the guy she'd loved tugged at her heart, and Mia swallowed hard.

The fire in Elliot's eyes was speaking to her, but she didn't know what he was trying to say. Her gaze flitted away from his face, unable to handle the intensity she saw there.

"I should probably get back," she said, her voice low and strained. "I've got to take over the front desk for a while this evening."

"I'm sorry, Mia," he said softly, his voice so low she leaned in without meaning to. He reached for her hand and she moved it away, but not before his fingers grazed her own. Shivers ran up her arms and sent a tremor through her shoulders.

Shaking her head slightly, she let out a shuddering breath. "It was six years ago, Elliot. It's time for me to let it go and move on. I can't hate you forever."

"You haven't moved on?" he asked, his lips forming a wicked smile as he grazed past her last comment.

"I've dated plenty of men," Mia countered. "I was implying that I needed to move on from my anger." And she did. It wasn't healthy to hold onto the pain so much. Whether she could let it go or not was irrelevant; the back and forth of their conversations in just the last two days had worn her out. It was time for a truce. Mia could handle a few more days with Elliot, and then he would go back to LA, and she could get back to her life. Inhaling, she offered him a smile. "It's in the past now. We can be friends."

He winced slightly and covered it quickly. But she'd noticed. "Friends," he agreed. "Cool. Hug it out?"

Mia had to chuckle as she shook her head. Friends was one thing. But physical contact? "I'm not sure—"

"A friend would totally hug me," he teased. "It's only weird if you make it weird."

He had a point. "Fine."

Elliot stepped forward, his hands coming around her back as she wrapped her arms around his waist. He felt much the same, only taller and broader. She tilted her head to look away from his face and rested her temple on his collar bone. Inhaling, Mia was immediately transported back in time to six years before by the spicy and masculine scent. She knew he didn't wear cologne, but that he used the same soap this many years later was surprising to her.

Enveloped in Elliot, Mia was suddenly overcome by the

strong desire to reach up on tip toes and kiss him, much as she would have when they'd dated years before.

She stilled. That thought had come out of nowhere, and it was not good.

Pulling herself from his grasp, Mia stepped back and allowed the cool air to wash over her from his distance. Offering him a strained smile, she said, "I'll see you around."

Elliot nodded, standing still as she turned to go. Picking up the projector box to put away, Mia promptly whistled for Pug. He jumped from the couch where he'd been snoozing for the duration of that interlude, and they left the room.

She felt Elliot's eyes like fire on her back until she stepped into the hall and out of sight.

CHAPTER NINE

Mia stood at the head of the long table in the Wasatch Room and surveyed her guests. She'd awoken that morning and checked on the roads, both disappointed and somewhat relieved that the bridge still wasn't fixed and her guests would have to remain for another day. They'd managed to clear the avalanche though, so she knew it would only be a matter of time until the road was repaired.

She had planned a cookie decorating activity for the late morning. Rosie had made almost one hundred sugar cookies in various shapes. Trees, candy canes, Santa faces and snowflakes all adorned the long table Mia had set up, surrounded by sprinkles and bowls of different colored frosting.

Mia took the supply of sprinkles Janice purchased for the Caldwell family activity, but she didn't think either the hotel owner or the Caldwell family would mind, given the circumstances.

The door sat propped open, and Ashlyn poked her head inside, grinning at Mia before snapping her gum.

"Unprofessional," Mia chided.

Ashlyn crossed the floor, rolling her eyes. "You know I don't do it when the guests are around."

"Maybe you could teach that tact to some of our fellow coworkers," Mia said under her breath.

"I heard that."

Mia ignored her friend's remark. "Want to decorate some cookies?"

"I'll take one to go, but I should probably stay at the desk."

"True," Mia conceded. And despite their joking, she knew Ashlyn did her best to remain professional when the situation warranted it.

Ashlyn picked up a plate and placed a snowflake cookie on it. She focused on spreading blue frosting over the cookie as she asked, "Any developments with our VIP guest?"

Mia stilled. "What do you mean?"

"Aside from annoying teenagers asking for a selfie, I mean. Has anyone bothered him? Personally, I wouldn't mind a selfie with *the* Brad Jenkins, but I know, I know. It's unprofessional."

Mia knew her friend was calling Elliot by his character's name on the show he starred in. She'd seen every episode, herself. Not that she would ever admit it to him.

"We've had no complaints," Mia said.

Ashlyn loaded her frosted cookie with sprinkles, then turned to go. "Keep me posted," she called before she disappeared.

The Kirkpatrick family filed into the room, and Mia greeted them, helping them to choose seats and get started on their decorating. Amy followed shortly with her husband and kids, and Mia had to force herself not to watch the door for Elliot to come behind them.

"Feeling better?" Mia asked Brandon as he chose a seat.

"Much," he said with feeling. "I think it was food poisoning. We left home early so we could spend the day in Salt Lake, and I think I must have eaten some bad tacos."

"Yikes," Mia said. "I'm glad you're well."

"Well and starving," Brandon said, eyeing the cookies.

A yapping dog ran into the room, barking at the tables and running underneath the guests' chairs. Mrs. Bruin's terrier was frantic, and Mia ran around the table to try and cut it off at the pass.

"Snookums!" Mrs. Bruin called, running into the room out of breath and glancing around with frenzied eyes for her dog.

Snookums? How had Mia not known the dog's name before now?

Elliot jogged into the room right after Mrs. Bruin, searching the room as well.

The terrier barked again from underneath the table and Mrs. Bruin moaned. "Oh, my Snookums!"

Getting on her hands and knees, Mia lifted the red vinyl tablecloth and located the small dog where he'd hid himself between two table legs.

"Come here, Snookums," Mia said, feeling both silly and helpless. The dog ignored her. "Snookums, *come*."

The little dog turned to look at her, and his beady, black eyes seemed to mock her. He barked once and she glared back, crawling underneath the table in between guest's legs to reach him.

As soon as she got within snatching distance, Mia reached for the terrier. He jumped away and out from under the table, yapping. She watched underneath the tablecloth as wrinkly hands reached down and grabbed Snookums, scooping him into the air. Mia backed out from under the table, apologizing to the Kirkpatrick family for the fiasco and for crawling on the floor near their feet.

"Don't worry about it," Mrs. Kirkpatrick said, smiling kindly with her eyes. "At least he didn't get the cookies."

Just as she spoke the words, the little dog leapt from Mrs. Bruin's arms and landed on the table, diving headfirst into a plate of Rosie's perfectly baked sugar cookies.

"Snookums, no!" Mrs. Bruin wailed.

Elliot reached over the seated guests and scooped up the little dog, pivoting away from the table and carrying Snookums straight out the door. Mrs. Bruin's worried gaze darted around the mess and the guest's faces before landing on the door and chasing after her dog.

Mia picked up the platter of dog-smooshed treats and swiped the additional crumbs onto it before turning toward the group. "Well, that was an adventure. Please feel free to decorate as many cookies as you are able to eat."

Turning away from the group, Mia carried the platter of crumbs and cracked pieces to the garbage and promptly dumped them in the trash. She then turned for the door and left at a calm pace, following the sound of Mrs. Bruin's wails until she located the woman sitting on one of the overstuffed chairs in the lobby which faced the Christmas tree. Snookums was in her lap, and she absently rubbed his back while Elliot appeared to be doing his best to soothe the older woman.

He glanced up as Mia approached, and they shared a look.

This woman needed to calm down. The dog had gotten loose, yes. And he had trampled a platter of cookies, yes. But no one got hurt.

Except for Elliot's ears as he had to sit and listen to this woman's moaning.

Mia approached them, and he was so grateful for her calming presence. "Mrs. Bruin, would you like to come to the kitchen with me for a cup of tea? I know we have peppermint in stock, which I heard you mention is your favorite flavor."

Mrs. Bruin brought her head up. "I would love tea," she

said. "But I think I would like to stay right here." She eyed Elliot in a way that proved exactly why she wanted to remain. Him. The older woman had developed a fancy for him, evidently.

"Of course," Mia said. "Let me run and make you a cup of tea, and I'll be back in a jiffy."

Elliot watched her leave, wishing he could go, too.

"You know, I've seen you somewhere before," Mrs. Bruin said, suddenly watching him with intent.

"Have you? How funny." Elliot lowered himself in the other overstuffed chair and glanced at the Christmas tree. It was simple, but nice. Someone had strung their popcorn and cranberry garland around part of the tree, which brought a smile to his lips. It was incongruent with the remainder of the decor, but it fit his idea of Christmas decorations well.

"Do you ever go to Seattle in the summertime?" Mrs. Bruin continued.

Elliot paused. The sitcom he starred in was based in Seattle. But he'd only been to the actual city once, and it had been during the fall.

"No," he said, shaking his head. "Is that where you're from?"

"Oh, yes," Mrs. Bruin said, petting her dog. "I come here each winter for the snow and then I go back home and enjoy Christmas with my rain."

"Perhaps I've seen you here then," Elliot said. "My family has spent Christmas in Hidden Hollow for the last five years. It's become a tradition for us as well."

"Perhaps," the older woman said, though she didn't look convinced. "Do you ski?"

Elliot hadn't heard that question in a while. He was asked constantly right after he moved to LA. The moment he would tell anyone he came from Utah, they automatically assumed he was a snow sports expert. And they weren't wrong.

Fortunately for him, he *didn't* ski. So he could answer the question honestly. "No. I've never skied in my life."

"Shame," Mrs. Bruin said, sighing. "I've always wished I'd learned."

Heels clicked through the foyer and Mia came around the corner, holding a mug and dipping a tea bag up and down in the steaming water. Mrs. Bruin accepted the tea and settled more comfortably in her chair before bringing the cup to her lips.

"I should get back to the activity," Mia said. "But can I get you anything else first?"

"I am just fine," Mrs. Bruin said, smiling contentedly. "Mr. James is here if I need anything."

Elliot glanced up and caught Mia's eye, careful to guard his expression before he gave away too much amusement. Mia lifted her eyebrows slightly and clasped her hands together, her smile restrained as though she was biting back laughter.

"Very well." Mia turned to go, and Elliot watched her walk across the foyer and around the corner toward the Wasatch Room.

"I think I'm going to enjoy this tea and then take myself upstairs for a nap."

"That sounds like a lovely way to pass the afternoon, Mrs. Bruin," Elliot said. He sat quietly by her side while she drank her tea and thought back to last year when his whole family had spent the day on the slopes, and he'd remained at the hotel "working."

He'd watched movies and snacked on mustard pretzels the entire day, wallowing in his own self-pity. For someone who got his start on television from being an inspiration to others, he really didn't know how to tap into that inspiration for himself. He'd broken his back and messed up his right leg so badly his doctors had told him he'd probably never walk again.

When he got up and took those first few steps eight months after the accident and a month before the Olympics, he'd been inundated with companies hoping to use his success story to sell their products.

He'd liked the dollar signs they threw at him, and had the hospital bills to pay, so naturally, he'd accepted.

Looking back on it now, he wondered if he ever would have said yes to repping that honey cereal had he known how things would have gone from there.

"Have a good day, Elliot," Mrs. Bruin said, pulling him from his reverie. She was standing in front of him, holding her dog in her arms like a baby, and she'd left her mug on the table between their chairs. How long had he been lost in thoughts of the past?

"I'm sure I'll see you around," he responded. Elliot waited until the woman was gone before standing. He was glad Mia had called a sort of truce between them. Things would be easier now.

But the hug he'd gotten from Mia had knocked him back a peg. The feel of her in his arms sparked a yearning within him, and he couldn't even think of it now without his chest aching. He had dated and loved·that woman for four years. Yes, they were young. But when he'd proposed to her, he'd meant it.

He just hadn't expected depression to swoop down on him like a black bird and darken his thoughts and his senses. When he'd ghosted Mia, he hadn't realized what he was doing. It wasn't until he was settled in LA and accepting the contract from the network that he realized his foolishness.

And now she was here and offering him friendship, and he wanted more. He wanted to try again. And to prove to her that the childish actions of six years ago weren't representative of the man he'd grown to be.

The only question was how?

CHAPTER TEN

Ashlyn sat behind the front desk, eyeing Mia as though she'd gone crazy. And maybe she had.

"If Janice was here, she wouldn't be throwing together all these activities and orchestrating group meals and sleeping in the hotel to make sure everyone was happy *at all times*."

Mia came around the counter and dropped into the rolly-chair beside her friend. "Are you trying to say I've lost my mind?"

"I am not trying. I am saying you've lost your mind. It's just a hotel, Mia."

"And it's my one shot to prove myself," Mia countered. "I can't keep being an assistant manager forever."

Ashlyn's light red eyebrows pulled together, her head tilting to the side. "You haven't even been here a full year."

"Correct. But it's my third hotel and my second round of being the assistant. I want to manage."

Ashlyn pulled a packet of gum from her purse underneath the desk. "I'm sure you will. Unless Janice is freaked out by your over-enthusiasm like the rest of us."

"Thanks for the support," Mia said wryly, reaching over to

steal a piece of gum. She removed the wrapper and popped it in her mouth.

Ashlyn was saving her money to go to cosmetology school in the city. She had dreams, but they didn't revolve around the hospitality business. She just didn't get it.

Mia wanted to succeed. She loved what she did, and she wanted to be even better. She got bursts of energy from successfully orchestrating the activities for the snowed-in guests or seeing people come together from different places to enjoy a meal who otherwise would have driven down to Park City and eaten at one of the restaurants there.

The elevator dinged and Mia looked up. Her shoulders deflated slightly when it was Mr. Kirkpatrick and his wife who stepped into the lobby. They waved on their way across the foyer and into the parlor.

"Who are you hoping to see?" Ashlyn asked.

"What?"

Ashlyn raised one eyebrow, pursing her lips with a slight shake of her head. "I'm not blind. Every single time the elevator opens you look at it quickly. And every time someone walks out, you're disappointed." She gasped quietly. "Oh my lanta. Have you taken a liking to our resident VIP?"

Mia wrinkled up her nose. "What? Ew."

Ashlyn chuckled, her mouth opening in delight. "You have! Your cheeks are turning pink. You like Elliot James, don't you?"

Mia glanced away. She felt her cheeks warming further at the insinuation. Ashlyn didn't know the half of it.

Ashlyn's voice lowered and she slapped her hand on the counter, her head dipping. "Oh my...you are being awfully quiet and bashful. Did something happen between you two?"

Mia's face whipped up. The last thing she needed was for rumors to spread among the staff that she'd been inappropriate with a guest. And a VIP guest, at that.

She'd lose the manager position for sure.

"No, it's not that. I know him," Mia admitted.

Ashlyn's eyes grew wide. "I know, right? You watch someone on TV for long enough and you totally feel like they're your best friend. And they are probably nothing in real life like their character, but you still think—"

"No, Ashlyn," Mia said. "I *know* him. We went to high school together."

Ashlyn's chin dropped. "You know Elliot James in real life and you didn't say anything?" Her eyes narrowed as if she had a hard time reconciling Mia's claim as the truth. "Then why didn't you tell me before?"

"Because it's not that big of a deal."

"Um, I beg to differ. He's like one of the hottest guys on TV right now." She raised her eyebrows. "Did he sign your yearbook? Because you could probably sell that thing for big money."

He more than signed her yearbook, but Mia wasn't about to admit to her previous serious relationship. Or that at one point she had referred to Elliot as her fiancé.

A shiver ran down her spine and shook her shoulders.

"Cold?" Ashlyn asked.

"A little," Mia lied. "I'm gonna run upstairs and grab a sweater. Are you still good with covering the front desk for a few extra hours? I think the guests will really like tonight's activity."

"Sure thing," Ashlyn said, turning toward the computer. Mia watched her friend locate Netflix and begin scanning the Christmas movies. Chuckling, she crossed the lobby and peeked out the window. Snow was still coming down in fast, heavy flakes. It was so thick Mia could hardly make out the buildings on the other side of the street. She'd watched someone drive through the road earlier in his truck with a plow attached to the front, but it was already covered again, and she was sure there was a heavy layer of ice underneath the innocent-looking blanket of powder. Either way, this snow was probably making it difficult on the crew trying to fix the bridge.

These guests weren't going anywhere today.

Swallowing, Mia turned for the stairwell, debating her options. Christmas was only two days away, so it was beginning to look like they might have to prepare to spend the holiday in the hotel.

Pausing on the second set of stairs, Mia closed her eyes and dropped her head back. She just had to be grateful the power had stayed on, and they never lost reception. Sure, they had a glitch the first night, but the generator had kicked right in and the power was back on by morning.

And they had plenty of food to get them through the holiday —minus fresh cranberries for the sauce, of course.

It could be worse. Mia counted her blessings and considered the situation a win, so far. If nothing else, Janice would be pleased with the way Mia had handled being snowed in with guests for that long. She hoped.

Even if some of the scheduled guests never arrived and the hotel was losing money each day. The *customer experience* was great. Mia needed to push that component when talking with her boss after this whole ordeal was over.

"Asleep standing up, eh?" a deep voice said in front of her. "You just keep surprising me with all these new skills."

A smile formed on Mia's face, and she opened her eyes to find Elliot standing before her on the landing. The dim stairwell was only lit by track lights at their feet and poorly glowing bulbs above, which cast shadows across his face and darkened his unshaven jaw.

He looked dangerous in the soft lighting, and Mia had to swallow a lump in her throat.

"What are you doing?" she asked, her hoarse voice echoing in the stairwell.

"I was trying to get downstairs. But the acting manager of

the hotel was standing in the center of my path, so I was waiting for her to move. Not that I'm complaining. I like the view."

She lifted her eyebrows, ignoring the delicious way Elliot's mouth formed a teasing smile. "You couldn't go down the elevator?"

His eyes darted away, an awkward chuckle escaping his mouth.

Mia knew that awkward chuckle. There was something he didn't want to share. She stepped a little closer, biting back her own smile. "What is it? Are you claustrophobic now?"

"What? No. It has nothing to do with small, enclosed spaces. If it did, I'd be uncomfortable right now."

He had a point. The stairwell was narrow and the two of them took up the entire landing on their own. "Then what is it?"

He shrugged. "I just don't want to be caught in the elevator if the power goes out again."

Mia pushed out her chin, nodding. "That's actually pretty reasonable."

Elliot's smile was back. "Have a little faith, Mia."

Then give me something to have faith in.

It was almost as if Elliot had read her mind, for a serious expression fell over his face. His voice fell to a low, throaty tone and he dipped his chin. "Mia, I am so sorry. I was such an idiot. I know I treated you horribly, and I should have at least tried to explain what was going on at the time."

"But you didn't," she said, her voice soft and small. Forget what she said about letting it go. One mention of that difficult time, and she felt like a nineteen-year-old all over again, crying in her dorm room and wondering what she'd done to ruin everything.

He gazed at her with a look so intense she simultaneously wanted to back up a step and jump into his arms.

But she couldn't move either direction. Her feet were rooted to the spot, her gaze glued to his face.

"There is no excuse for my behavior," he said, imploring her with his gaze, "but you need to know I take full responsibility for my actions. I've regretted them for years. After you told me never to call you again, I had to respect that, but I see now that I should have kept trying—"

"Hold on," Mia said, confusion clouding Elliot's apology. She lifted a hand to stall his words, shaking her head. "I never told you anything. I haven't spoken to you since you *proposed*."

"I know. I don't mean *you*, exactly. I mean when your mom told me what you'd said."

Mia's body went cold, and she tried to make sense of his words. "Refresh my memory. When was this?"

"On the phone. During the Olympics. A year after the accident."

"So right after you moved to LA."

Elliot nodded. "When I called to talk and your mom answered your phone. She told me you couldn't bear to speak with me, and it was better if we just let things go."

Mia felt like she'd been hit on the head with a broomstick. Her brain was going fuzzy and her knees weak. She turned, squeezing past Elliot in the hall and climbing the stairs toward the second floor.

"Wait," he called. "Where are you going?"

"I have some things to do," Mia said, opening the door to the second floor and closing it behind her with a final click.

She needed to sort out the story Elliot just fed her. Because it sounded like he was saying he'd tried to make amends. And it really sounded like he claimed that Mia's own mother had put a stop to it.

But that didn't make any sense, because her mom was there on the front row for Mia's entire heartbreak. She heard Mia say over and over again that she never wished to see Elliot again, but she desired with every fiber of her being to receive some closure.

What reason would her mother have had for standing in the way of Mia getting the answers she so desperately wanted?

None. She would have exactly no good reason.

Mom had some explaining to do.

Elliot stood in the stairwell looking up to the second-floor landing where Mia had disappeared. What had he said that bothered her so much?

He'd been pleased with the way the conversation had been going. She was really listening, and he had been gearing himself up to explain the depth of his depression and the way it had affected every aspect of his life during that time, when she'd suddenly turned and left.

Had it been too much for her? Shaking out his arms, Elliot turned for the main floor again. He'd been headed to the parlor to check out the small lending library he'd heard Mrs. Kirkpatrick speaking about when he ran into Mia. He'd checked with the hotel's handyman earlier that day for an update on the broken road and if he had to guess, he'd assume they were spending another day or two in the hotel.

Which included Christmas.

Not that he was complaining. He would have preferred to be with his parents and the rest of his family, but he was enjoying the Powder Peaks Lodge thus far. Mia had gone above and beyond utilizing her skills and some of his parents' unused activities to create an enjoyable week for the patrons who would rather be out snowboarding or home with their rainy Seattle weather.

Although, if Elliot had his guess, he'd assume Mrs. Bruin was just as happy in a free hotel room near Park City as she would have been at home.

Chuckling to himself, Elliot opened the door to the lobby.

"Mr. James," the friendly receptionist called from her desk. She gave him a wide smile. "Anything I can do for you?"

"I'm just checking out the books," he said.

"Wow." She looked surprised. "An actor who likes to read. That's pretty sweet."

Did she expect him to appreciate the slight? It certainly wasn't a compliment.

"So, I heard something interesting today," she continued, forcing him to stop walking and turn toward the desk.

He slung his hands in his pockets and read her name tag. "Yeah?"

"Yeah," Ashlyn said around her chewing gum. "I heard you used to know my boss."

He froze. Had Mia said something? "The old woman?" he asked, in case Mia hadn't divulged their relationship.

Ashlyn laughed. "Janice isn't that old. But no, Mia. Mia Murphy? I thought you two went to high school together?"

Elliot tried not to feel disappointed that that was all Mia had said about their connection. But he supposed that was better than telling everyone he was a liar and a horrible person. Though he knew Mia well enough to know she wouldn't purposefully spread hurtful things about his character. She'd had six years to go to the tabloids with the story of the way he'd treated her, and never once had it leaked.

"Yeah," he confirmed. "I've known her since kindergarten, actually. She used to wear these super big bows around her pigtails that were almost bigger than her head. But you didn't hear that from me." He shot Ashlyn a wink, and she smiled like he'd handed her the keys to his Porsche.

"Were you two friends?" she asked, leaning forward and lowering her voice.

"I'd like to think so," Elliot said.

"Oh my lanta," Ashlyn said, shaking her head. "I can't believe she never told me. All this time I've drooled over you on *My Crazy Family*, and she never once mentioned you grew up together."

Elliot had to chuckle over her mention of drool. He'd heard it a few times before, and it never ceased to make him feel insanely awkward.

"Tell me," Ashlyn said, leaning even closer. "What is Sophy Grant like?"

Elliot paused, doing his best not to roll his eyes. "She's a really talented actress," he said diplomatically. He wasn't about to reveal that Sophy was a spoiled brat who put off production more than he'd like to put up with, and the first date they went on was completely ruined because it began to rain and Sophy was deathly afraid of lightning.

Ashlyn's eyes went round. "She really is. And to think, you get to play her brother on TV. I can't believe you're staying in my hotel."

"Well, I better get going. I was just going to look at the books..."

Ashlyn sat up straight, shaking her head as if she was recalling where she was and what she was doing. "Right. Sorry. I shouldn't have bothered you. Go ahead and browse the books in the parlor, Mr. James, and feel free to take whatever you'd like."

Elliot did just that. He found an old Louis L'Amour book he hadn't read since high school and slid it from the shelves. Passing Ashlyn on his way back to the stairs, Elliot lifted his hand in farewell.

"Mr. James?" she called.

He swallowed a groan. "What's up?"

"You won't tell Mia that I bugged you, right? I'm sorry. I fangirled for a minute and lost my head."

Elliot could hear the sincerity in her tone, and he liked her for it. Something about her request made him feel like she was less afraid of getting in trouble and more concerned with not disappointing Mia.

He could understand that sentiment.

"I won't say a word."

CHAPTER ELEVEN

The line rang over and over again in Mia's ear before going to voicemail. She clicked the phone off and tossed it on her bed.

She'd tried calling her mom six times. And six times, the phone had sent her to voicemail. What could her mother possibly be doing that was more important than answering Mia's call?

It was probably a good thing Mia hadn't spoken to her mom right away after the conversation with Elliot in the stairwell, because the hour of calling had given her plenty of time to cool down and consider the situation. She was less furious now and more willing to consider that there might be a reasonable explanation.

Chimes went off in the room, and Mia dove for her phone, she reached for it so quickly. Sliding it on, she clicked the speakerphone button right away.

"Mom. I have questions."

"Well hello, honey. First tell me that you're safe."

"I'm safe," Mia said.

Her mom sighed into the phone. "Thank heavens. I saw all

your missed calls and nearly had a heart attack. How's the bridge repair coming along?"

Mia would have felt guilty if she wasn't feeling so high strung. "Fine. They are working on it. And we have plenty of electricity, blankets and food." She drew in a breath. "Mom, we need to talk. I had a conversation with Elliot James, and it confused me. I need you to straighten out an accusation he made."

The phone was so silent Mia had to check it to make sure it was still on. "Mom?" she asked.

"Yes, I'm here." Mom cleared her throat, and Mia could hear her walking into another room and closing the door, for the din of voices in the background lowered to nothing. "What is it?"

"Elliot said he called me a year after the accident, and you told him I didn't want to hear from him ever again. But that's crazy because you *knew* I wanted to hear from him."

The phone was silent again, and a small amount of dread began to build in Mia's stomach. "Mom?" she asked, her anxiety growing with each passing quiet second.

"Yes," Mom said softly. "It's true."

It was Mia's turn to be silent. She gave her mom a moment to continue but when the silence stretched further, she couldn't help but blurt out, "Why? You knew I wanted closure."

"I was trying to protect you."

Mia scoffed. "Oh, what is this? A cheesy movie? The nineteenth century? This doesn't actually happen in *real life*, Mom. Trying to protect me? You can't be serious."

"Well I am. You were home for the weekend and left your phone in the house when you went out with your dad to see his new horse or goat or whatever new animal he had at the time, and Elliot called. I was so shocked I answered the phone, and when he asked to speak with you, the words just came out of my mouth."

Mia guarded her tongue from biting back and merely asked, "What words?"

"I told him to leave you be. I said you were happy and had moved on and it would only make things difficult if he tried to contact you again. I told Elliot you desired to never speak to him again. And then I made him promise to leave you alone."

Mia dropped the phone onto her lap, the wall blurring as her eyes went out of focus. "Did he say what he was calling about?"

"What? Mia honey, I can't hear you. You sound so far away."

Mia lifted the phone closer to her mouth. "I asked if he said what he was calling about."

"No. I didn't ask. I just cut him off at the pass. And I did it for you, Mia. You were just barely starting to get out there and go on dates, and I didn't want him to derail you again. You couldn't afford to fail any more classes, or you would have lost your internship at the hotel. And look how fabulously that turned out."

"Yeah," she agreed absently, looking around the hotel she was currently sitting inside and then down at the phone. It wasn't the hotel she'd interned with, but that position had springboarded her career. "I've gotta go."

"Mia, are you feeling all right?"

"Yes," she said quickly. "I just need to go."

"Call me later, please."

"Sure." Mia slid the phone off and tossed it on the bed. She didn't want to be that girl who was hung up on what-ifs, but in the moment, she couldn't help it. Elliot had called.

He had *called*. All of those years of hating him for ghosting her when he *had* tried to make an effort and reached out. And Mia never knew.

She felt an overwhelming desire to pick up one of the fluffy pillows on her bed and scream into it. But then her phone beeped, and she reached for it instead. She found a text from Ashlyn.

The carolers have gathered.

Shoot. She needed to get downstairs right away. Groaning, Mia typed back a reply that she was on her way and slid her phone into her pocket. Now was not the time to worry about the past and the things she couldn't change. Now was the time for focusing on the job she wanted at the end of this disastrous week and the things she was doing to create a memorable holiday—and hopefully a few five-star Yelp reviews—for her snowed-in guests.

She checked on Pug, where he was fast asleep in his little bed on the floor, and then quickly changed out his water dish.

Rushing down the stairs and to the lobby, Mia was instantly gratified to find every guest from the hotel gathered around the Christmas tree. All they needed was a piano to sing around and it truly would have felt like being home for the holidays.

But this was better than nothing.

Not to mention the fact that at the moment, she didn't feel like being home anyway.

Elliot stood beside his brother-in-law on the outside of the group, and he glanced up as she approached, catching her eye. His green eyes were deep and familiar, entreating her. Mia held his gaze, unable to ignore the nagging thought in the back of her mind: *what if she had answered the phone instead of her mother when he'd called all those years ago?*

What ifs and regrets slithered around her stomach, and she forced her gaze away from Elliot. But she couldn't help the thought which swirled on repeat in her mind: *he'd called.*

"Welcome everyone," Mia said with forced cheerfulness. "Have you all had a chance to look over the music?"

Nods and murmuring joined in the general consensus that most everyone who wanted to had glanced through their music options.

She clapped her hands together in front of her. "Great. Let's get started. If we want to form a semicircle, let's have all of the men on this side" —she gestured to her left— "and altos here in the middle with sopranos on this side."

Groups began to break up and the commotion of everyone trying to find their places smoothed out into a semblance of a semicircle, with the exception of the kids on the end beside their mom.

Boston looked around himself for a minute as though he realized he was surrounded by women. Mia approached the child and squatted down to his level. "Did you want to go stand by your dad?"

Boston nodded.

She pointed to where Brandon stood beside Elliot at the far end of the men's side and her heart squeezed when the boy's eyes lit up. There was something very sweet about a little boy who loved his dad so dearly.

Boston zoomed past Mia and bowled into his dad's legs, inciting laughter among a few of the guests. Bringing herself to a stand, Mia exchanged an appreciative smile with Amy before taking the conductor's place once again.

"Bear with me," she said with a bit of a laugh. "I am not practiced at leading music. But I think we can get along fine."

"My wife runs the choir in our church back home," Mr. Kirkpatrick announced proudly.

Mia found Mrs. Kirkpatrick in the group, the woman's cheeks growing round and pink from the attention. "Would you like to lead us?"

"If you need me to, I would be more than happy to help."

And Mia felt more than happy to sit back and let someone handle things who knew what she was doing. "Please," she said, gesturing to the front, "come direct us."

The women traded places and Mrs. Kirkpatrick immediately delivered a wide smile to the group. "Shall we begin with *Jingle Bells* to warm up our voices?"

She brought her hands up and Mia almost flinched when

Mrs. Kirkpatrick began leading; her arms waved wildly, shaking and cutting through the air as if she was throwing magic around the room.

With the way their voices were melding so beautifully, and with the perfect sequence of songs Mrs. Kirkpatrick led the group through, Mia almost wondered if her short, enthusiastic arms did hold a bit of Christmas magic within them.

Music from the season filled the foyer as all of the guests got into the spirit of caroling. Even Ashlyn left the reception area and joined them after a few songs.

Mia sang along to her favorite carols, her gaze moving from the large, decorated tree before them to the windows flanking it with big, fat snowflakes falling lazily on the other side. She felt warm from the heater and the bodies surrounding her, but a warmth filled Mia's soul that wasn't caused by the thermostat.

They ended on *Silent Night, Holy Night* and Mia brought her finger up to catch a lone tear which had gathered in the corner of her eye. Putting on a smile, she thanked everyone for attending and participating and announced that hot cocoa and pastries would be served in the dining room.

Boston and Taylor ran for the hallway and their parents hastily followed behind them. The remainder of the guests slowly filed toward the dining room, Ashlyn among them, but Mia stood beside the tree, her hands clasped softly in front of her and her heart aching for home.

It was easy to say she was fine missing Christmas with her parents because the opportunity at work was too good to pass up. But *actually* missing Christmas with her family? She was unprepared for how much she would wish to be home, regardless of how irritated she was with her mom at the moment. She was still her mom.

"I think that was a success," Elliot said, sidling up beside her. "Mrs. Kirkpatrick could take her skills national."

"She certainly has a lucky church choir," Mia agreed.

Elliot's hand slid across her back, causing Mia to grow still. He cupped her far shoulder and brought her close to his side in a tight, one-armed hug. Mia had to fight the temptation to lean her head against him.

His thumb started rubbing small circles on her shoulder bone and Mia sighed, relenting.

In another life, this would have been her husband. In another life, they could have had kids by now to sing carols and decorate cookies with. In another life...Mia shook her head. She couldn't keep doing this to herself. She could only move forward.

But, *he had tried to call.*

Turning her head, she gave Elliot a soft smile. "I'm glad you're here."

CHAPTER TWELVE

S he was glad he was there. Never in a million years did Elliot think he would hear those words. And yet, he could see in her gorgeous blue eyes that she'd meant it.

Now how did he agree with her without scaring her away?

Releasing her shoulder, Elliot faced her head on. "Mia, what do you have planned for tomorrow?"

Her eyes flicked away from him and a guilty smile fell over her lips. "You don't have to participate in all of the activities."

"I want to," he said, unable to tear his gaze away from her mouth. "What is it?"

"Um, well...I was planning to announce a ski trip for tomorrow." She continued, talking fast as if she wanted to spit out all of the information at once. "I know we can't get down to Park City but there's a few good runs up the mountain here and if a few people are willing to ferry others up via snowmobiles we could get some good skiing in. But obviously I don't expect you to join us on this outing. And I contemplated changing it to something else, but really...most people come to Park City for the snow."

His gut wrenched at the thought of strapping on another snowboard.

She gave him a regretful smile. "I'm sorry, Elliot."

"No," he said at once, shaking his head. "Don't apologize. It's not a huge deal."

Mia didn't look convinced. The energy moving between them was stilted, and Elliot was sure neither of them was saying what they really felt.

"I better get to the dining room," Mia said, taking a step away. "Are you coming in for hot cocoa?"

His pocket began to sing an instrumentalized version of *Feliz Navidad,* and he pulled his phone out, reading the name on the screen. He glanced up at Mia. "It's my dad. I better take this."

"Great, I'll see you later then."

He watched Mia walk away. He wanted to sing praises aloud for her change in attitude toward him, but he also didn't want to sound like a crazy man, so he kept his mouth closed.

Answering his phone, he put it up to his ear. "Hey, Dad."

"Elliot, what's going on with those mountain roads? Can you make it down to Park City now?"

Turning to face the window, Elliot scanned the opposite side of Main Street and the dark windows lining the buildings. The town had become eerie since he'd arrived, almost like a ghost town. He realized that it was due, in part, to a lot of the people living on the other side of the broken bridge and not being able to cross into town to work, but he didn't mind it. He didn't mind not being able to eat at the other restaurants or shop in the boutique stores.

His last few days being stuck primarily within the lodge had been some of the best days he'd had in a while.

"Elliot?"

"Sorry Dad," he said, turning his attention back to the phone. "I got distracted. But I'm not sure what's going on. A guy that works at the hotel has a friend on the crew that's repairing the bridge, so he'll let us know the moment we're able to pass over it. He really doesn't think it'll be much longer."

"Good. Your mom is hoping we can be reunited in time for Christmas."

Elliot smiled. "I hope so too, Dad. I'll keep you posted."

He hung up the phone and slid it into his pocket. He wished he could be with his family, but he was enjoying his time in the lodge. And until he was forced to leave, he was going to spend every spare minute he could doing his best to convince Mia to give him another shot.

With determination, Elliot turned away from the window and the Christmas tree. He was going to go find Mia and have some hot cocoa with her.

The Kirkpatrick kids were leaning against the back wall of the lodge beside their dad, all decked out in their snow clothes, while their mom took a photo of them. Elliot waited patiently at the snowmobiles for them to finish with the photo op, sunlight streaming down over them and lighting the glittery snow. The lodge backed up into the mountain and there was nothing but forest and sloping mountainside behind them.

This was part of the reason his family chose Hidden Hollow every year for their Christmas retreat and not Park City. It was remote. They could appreciate the perks of a hotel while simultaneously feeling like they were inhabiting a log cabin in the woods.

Elliot checked his watch. Mia had told him to meet her at the top ten minutes ago. They needed to head out. The teenage daughter, Erin, glanced up from her place beside her dad and brother, and her scheming eyes settled on Elliot.

She was going to ask for another picture.

He stepped forward at once and Erin's eyes brightened. She was in for a little disappointment. He didn't mind taking selfies with fans, but Erin had been taking photos and videos of him constantly over the last few days. She had plenty in her phone already. And they were late.

"Mrs. Kirkpatrick," he called, crossing the distance. "We've really got to get a move on. But if you'd like me to snap a photo of your family really quickly, I'd love to."

Mrs. Kirkpatrick beamed at him, reaching forward with her phone. "Thank you, that would be lovely."

Sidling up beside her husband, Mrs. Kirkpatrick rested her hand on his chest and smiled at Elliot. Erin frowned on her other side and Elliot took one shot of the girl's irritated face before calling, "Smiles, everyone."

Erin got the hint. Elliot snapped the photo and then reached forward to give the phone back. "We better head out. Mr. Kirkpatrick, I was told you know how to operate a snowmobile?"

"Indeed, young man."

"Great." Elliot reached forward and slapped their teenage son on the back. "I can take this guy on mine. Let's head out."

They climbed onto the snowmobiles, the teenagers holding the snowboards as they rode on the back. Mia was already at the top with Amy, Brandon, and their kids. She'd explained where to go and Elliot thought he could handle helping the Kirkpatricks get there.

If only he'd known that they'd want a twenty-minute photo session first.

He looked over his shoulder to make sure Mr. Kirkpatrick was behind him, then turned up the mountain, following the tracks Mia and his family members had left behind. Within minutes they reached the top of Hidden Hollow's best rugged terrain slope and found the snowmobiles parked off to the side while the kids rolled large balls of snow with their dad. Mia and

Amy were walking back from the tree line toward Brandon and the kids.

"Who wants to learn how to snowboard?" Elliot called, taking off his helmet and leaving it on the seat.

"Me!" Taylor yelled, dropping the sticks she'd gathered and jumping up and down. Boston looked a little more hesitant, but Elliot would ease him into it.

Elliot picked up Taylor, swinging her through the air. "Are you excited?"

"Yes," she said through peals of giggles. "I'm going to be a USA qualifier someday."

Elliot set her on the ground and flicked the puffy ball on top of her hat. "I'm sure you'll be great, Tay. It's in your blood."

Boston looked up from the snowman face he was creating. "Is it in my blood too?"

"Sure is, bud," Brandon said, shooting Elliot a grin. "You ready, man?"

Elliot nodded. He'd agreed to come up and help ferry the boarders in the snowmobiles, but he'd made it clear he wasn't getting on a snowboard.

Of course, when Amy hinted at him helping the kids learn with the new snowboards Brandon had bought them, Elliot had a hard time saying no. He didn't have to get on a board himself, just help them. And he was kind of looking forward to it.

Part of him also felt like throwing up, but that was beside the point.

His body grew physically ill whenever he thought back to that day when he'd taken the half pipe down and attempted a backside 720 melon grab. He remembered flying through the air wrong, the searing pain from hitting the ice, and then waking up later in the hospital bed with a broken back and a ruined leg.

His doctor had told him he'd never walk normally again. But he'd been wrong.

That didn't mean Elliot was eager to get back onto the

slopes. Even now, six years later, the idea of snowboarding caused him anxiety.

"How does it work?" Taylor asked, carrying over her brand new, hot pink snowboard and dropping it onto the snow at Elliot's feet. Her boots were already on and her dad had gotten click-ins, so Elliot showed her how to position her feet to snap her boots into the bindings.

Taylor reached forward and clutched Elliot's forearms, her smile as wide as her eyes while she gripped her uncle and slid on the snow.

Brandon approached them, carrying Boston in one arm and a tiny black and green snowboard in the other. He set his son on the ground and helped his boots into the bindings before sending Elliot a thumbs up.

Mia and Amy sat ready on two of the snowmobiles as the Kirkpatrick family prepared to ski down the mountainside. The women had agreed to ferry people back up to the top and Elliot was meant to help them when the lessons for his niece and nephew were through.

His gaze fixed on Mia while she pulled her helmet over her beanie-capped head. Her puffy white coat encased her like a marshmallow, and he wanted to run across the snow and tackle her into the thick powder, maybe incite a snowball fight like they'd done when they were younger. She glanced up and sent him a smile, and his heart flipped over in his chest.

"All right, guys," Elliot said, clapping his cold hands together and focusing his attention back on his niece and nephew. "The very first thing I am going to teach you is how to fall the right way."

CHAPTER THIRTEEN

All Mia could hear from where she sat on the snowmobile
next to Amy's was peals of giggles from Taylor and
Boston. They hadn't done much in the ten minutes since Elliot
began teaching them except fall on their bottoms, but Mia had
to assume Elliot knew what he was doing.

He used to be a professional snowboarder, after all.

"I can do the first few runs on my own," Mia said, leaning
closer to Amy. "I understand if you'd rather stay and watch the
lesson."

Amy didn't take her eyes off her brother, husband, and children as she wrinkled her nose and shook her head slightly. "I
don't mind helping out. I was just hoping Elliot would ride with
the kids. I was kind of waiting for that."

Mia debated asking the invasive question which bounced
around her head, but finally decided to keep silent. Elliot had
been fairly open with her since arriving at Powder Peaks. If she
wanted more details about the accident, she could ask him.

"Ready?" she asked.

Amy nodded, pulling her helmet on and revving up the
snowmobile. They took off single-file down the mountain,

passing the snowboard lessons and sending the giggling children a gloved wave.

They took the same path down the mountain which they'd used to get up and found the three Kirkpatricks waiting near the clearing behind the lodge.

"Who wants to go first?" Mia asked, approaching Mr. Kirkpatrick and his kids. Erin didn't look pleased. She unbuckled her boots and left her snowboard on the ground before stomping toward the lodge.

"My daughter is finished for the day," Mr. Kirkpatrick explained, reaching forward to pick up Erin's discarded snowboard.

"Then we can take you both," Amy said brightly. They drove the skier and his snowboarding son up the mountain and dropped them at the top before heading back to the bottom to wait. The cycle continued for another hour until Amy leaned over and said, "How much longer do you think we'll do this? We could have recruited Mr. Kirkpatrick's wife if we knew how long he'd want to go for."

"Maybe we can give them a final run and then call it quits," Mia said. "I should probably get back inside anyway."

They warned the Kirkpatricks and took them up to the top of the mountain, before dropping them off and watching them disappear into the powder again.

"How is the lesson going?" Amy called, turning off her snowmobile and leaving her helmet on the seat.

Mia hesitated. She was interested to see how the kids were doing, too, but she really did need to get back to the hotel to check on things. And by now the crew probably had an update on the bridge—something she was sure Janice would want to be notified of the moment it cleared.

But then Elliot looked up from holding his nephew's hand as they rode down the miniature slope area and his eyes shone like a beacon, calling to Mia and drawing her in. She followed behind Amy, approaching the men and kids and watching Brandon and Elliot help Taylor and Boston down little practice runs.

"I think you guys are ready to show these ladies what you can do," Elliot said, looking into each of their faces with confidence. "Who wants to show off?"

"Me!" Taylor and Boston yelled in unison. They each unclipped one boot and did an awkward walk-slide up the side of their smaller slope.

Once they reached the top, they both fell onto their bottoms and clicked in their boots like they'd been doing it for years. Amy looked impressed.

Brandon and Elliot positioned themselves at the bottom of the slope, their arms outstretched as though they waited at the end of a slide at the playground instead of an open, snowy mountainside.

The kids made tiny little jumps in the air until they were moving, albeit slowly, down toward the men. Both of their small faces were red from the cold but they were clearly elated.

"Well done!" Amy shouted, running to hug her kids once they reached the end of their route. "I'm so proud of you guys."

Boston had fallen before he reached his uncle, but Taylor had made it all the way to her dad in one smooth ride, and she was jumping up and down in the snow, squealing.

"I did it!" she yelled.

"Yes you did, sweetheart," Brandon said, picking her up and giving her a hug.

She turned toward Elliot. "Thank you, Uncle Elliot! Now I'm ready for the Olympics, right?"

Mia couldn't help but chuckle. She noted Elliot's warm smile and how it did not dim at the mention. He'd come a long way, from what she'd heard. The group came together, and the general consensus was that it was freezing, and everyone needed hot chocolate.

Loading up on the snowmobiles, Brandon and Amy took off right away with their kids on the back while Elliot bundled the snowboards together and tried securing them to the back seat of his snowmobile with a bungee cord.

Mia waited, watching him try and fail over and over again to get the hooks on the cord to connect. He finally dropped his hands and let everything fall into the snow, shooting Mia a look of such complete frustration she laughed.

"Need some help?" she offered.

"Please."

Taking her helmet off to make it easier to see, Mia crossed the distance and picked up the bungee cord from the snow, wrapping the small snowboards and tying them off right away.

"You made it look so difficult," she teased.

He lifted his hands, showing her bright red, bare fingers. "My fingers are ice," he explained, a rueful smile on his face.

The smile immediately slid off of Mia's face. "What on earth were you thinking, Elliot?"

"I was thinking that I didn't bring any snow gloves, but I wasn't about to miss the chance to teach my niece and nephew to board. I used some cotton gloves, but they soaked through pretty fast."

Mia shook her head. "That was downright reckless. There's no way you're driving back down. I can't afford to let you wreck a snowmobile."

He held her gaze, his clear eyes firmly trained on her. "And here I thought you were concerned for my safety."

She chuckled. "Yeah, I guess I don't want the hotel to be liable for your injuries, either. You better ride down with me."

"What about the other snowmobile?"

"I'll grab Marco and come back to get it. You can't control a throttle like that." She indicated his hands. "How will you even hold on? Maybe we should walk."

"I can manage," he said, and he began walking toward Mia's snowmobile.

She caught up and slid her helmet onto her head. Swinging her leg around, she sat down and waited for Elliot to sit behind her. When he finally swung onto the seat, she had to tell herself to breathe normally.

It wasn't the first time she'd driven Elliot on a snowmobile. But it certainly hadn't occurred in the last six years.

"Don't go too fast," he said into her ear.

"Hey, I'm a safe driver," she defended.

Elliot's laugh rang out around her and Mia turned on the seat, pausing when her shoulder lodged into Elliot's chest and she realized just how close they sat to one another. Swallowing, she gazed into his eyes and read an emotion there that she couldn't decipher. It wasn't sorrow or joy, it was an odd mix of the two.

Or so it appeared within the helmet secured on his head.

"Thanks for being a good sport out here," she said.

The look grew deeper, and Mia gazed into his eyes, doing her best to guess what he was thinking.

"I didn't realize how much I would enjoy it," he said at last, amusement filtering in and taking over his features. "I love those kids, but that aside, I had a lot of fun. Probably the most fun I've had in a really long time."

Mia scoffed. "You're a TV star. I'm sorry, Elliot, but I have a hard time believing that."

He shook his head. His voice sounded muffled against the helmet. "I'm sick of all that. I never really wanted it in the first place; I just liked the money they offered me."

Well, she hadn't expected to hear that. Nodding, Mia turned back around. She reached to start the snowmobile when Elliot's icy hand gripped her arm, stopping her.

"Listen," he said, his voice no longer muffled. She looked over her shoulder to find that he'd removed his helmet.

Mia removed hers as well.

His worried gaze raked over her, and he cleared his throat. "After the accident I got really sick."

"You mean beyond breaking your bones and going through rehab to learn to walk again?" Mia asked.

Elliot glanced away before settling his eyes back on her. "Yes. I don't mean physically. I mean mentally."

Mia sucked in a surprised breath, her body going still. She understood what *mentally sick* implied, but not when it related to Elliot James. He was the happiest, kindest man she knew. Aside from when he had dropped her like a hot rock, of course.

She swung her leg over the snowmobile so she was sitting sideways and was better able to see Elliot's face. This didn't feel like a short conversation. This was something that needed to be discussed.

CHAPTER FOURTEEN

Mia faced him, and Elliot was sure it was her way of showing him that she was ready to listen. He still straddled the snowmobile but there was plenty of room between them, so he didn't bother moving sideways like she had.

Mia sat still, waiting patiently for him to continue. He gathered his courage, playing with the chin strap of the helmet which sat in his lap. Drawing in a breath, he spoke before he could overthink things and convince himself to keep quiet.

"I became massively depressed," he said, watching Mia closely for her reaction. When her gaze didn't waver, he continued. "It crept on slowly, but I think it began the moment I woke up in the hospital and realized my dreams were crushed."

Her eyebrows pulled together and her tiny nose scrunched up. "But the epiphany—"

"Right," he said, trying to figure out the best way to explain what had happened to him. "I did mean that. I did feel like we could make a whole new life together and find our own joy without the Olympics. But I hadn't expected to be swallowed so wholly by despair. When the depression took over, I lost control over my feelings and my actions. I don't know how to explain it except that I was in a state of perpetual fog, of neverending apathy."

She shook her head. "Why didn't you tell me? I would have supported you and stood beside you through everything. I would have waited as long as you needed me to."

"And I can see that now, but when I was in the middle of the darkness, nothing would've convinced me that I was worth it. Especially you. I pushed you away, Mia, because I loved you so much. I knew you deserved better than what I could give you."

Her eyes were pained. "Until you called," she argued, her voice soft and small.

He swallowed. "That wasn't until a year later. My parents made me see a therapist and she helped me work through the situational depression while the physical therapists helped me walk again. By the time I left Utah to film those commercials, I was beginning to creep out of the haze."

"So...when you called?"

"When I called, I had just signed with an agent and was talking with the network about *My Crazy Family*." Elliot drew in a breath and spoke his truth. "I signed on with the show to pay back my parents for the crazy medical expenses my accident accrued. But I don't love acting, I just have a knack for it. I never expected the show to take off the way it did, and I never intended to be on TV forever."

Mia shook her head, her gaze clouded. "I just need a minute to wrap my head around this."

"And you can never know how many times over the years I've wanted to call you, but I tried to respect your wishes—"

"You should have called," she said.

Elliot stilled. What did she mean by that? Would she have welcomed him if he had reached out to her?

Mia looked into his eyes, her own crystal clear and sparkling from the winter sun. "I never asked my mom to tell you any of those things, Elliot. She just said those things in a misguided effort to protect me and then probably deleted the call. I never even knew."

Her words crashed over him like a giant snowball, a sharp realization that the truth he'd known for the last few years wasn't even true. Mia hadn't wanted him to leave her alone. If her words now were any indication, she would have welcomed Elliot had he reached out to her again. After he apologized and explained, of course. He lifted one red, icy hand up to her face and trailed it along her cheekbone.

Her cheeks were rosy, but still warmer than his hands, and she winced.

"Sorry," he said, pulling away.

Mia tugged her gloves off and picked up his hand. Her eyes met his and her eyebrows rose. "We should probably get you back to the lodge."

"In a minute," he said, his voice hoarse.

He watched as Mia did her best to shove her gloves over his frozen hands. They were definitely too small, but they were better than nothing. The soft fur lining was warm from Mia's hands and he felt the soothing heat start to work its magic over his fingers.

"Do you still struggle with depression?" she asked, her attention on his hands.

"Occasionally," he said honestly. "Mostly when I'm home-sick. LA is fine, but I miss my family, and I'm not doing something I love."

Mia quirked a smile. "You're a TV star. Most people would want to be in your shoes."

"It's not as glamorous as it seems. I was happier today than I've been in years." And he was choosing to examine the reasons for that at a later, more secluded time.

Mia tilted her head. "Because you spent time with your family? Or because you were playing in the snow?"

Or he could examine the reasons now. He glanced away from Mia, his eyes trailing the snow-capped peaks in the distance and the powdery trees. Family was important to him, even if they didn't choose to fill him in on every detail of their lives. Elliot nearly scoffed as he thought of his older brother, who had failed to mention that his kid was graduating early with a full ride to the University of Utah.

But as much as he loved his family, he knew that wasn't the main reason he'd been so happy today.

"It was the kids," he said, drawing his attention back to Mia. "I loved teaching them to snowboard. And while I was teaching them, I got this strange desire to strap on a board and ride down the mountain. Which is *crazy* since that idea has given me anxiety for the last six years."

"Maybe it's time to try again."

Elliot shook his head. "I don't know. But either way it's progress."

She cast him a warm smile.

He brought his hands up, encased in too-small gloves, and cupped Mia's cheeks. "Mia, will you give me another chance? No one has ever come close to filling my heart the way you have. You were the standard by which I've judged all other women in my life, and compared to you, everyone else fails."

"Sophy Grant?" Mia said, arching her eyebrow. Elliot's words were nice and all, but she had a hard time believing he preferred her over a TV superstar. And while the magic of his touch and his soothing words was uncoiling the tightly wound fence around her heart, she couldn't just ignore the life he had in LA.

Elliot rolled his eyes, dropping his hands from her face to his lap. "Why does everyone constantly bring her up? She was a fling, and it didn't last because she's crazy. No," he said, training his gaze on Mia, "Sophy Grant doesn't measure up to you. Now, what do you say?"

Mia's heart raced. Elliot was asking for something that she desperately wanted to give him: another chance.

And yet, she was scared. He'd gone off the deep end before and dropped her without a word or a chance for her to defend herself or fight for him. What was to say he wouldn't do it again?

She cleared her throat. "How can I know it won't happen again?"

"You can't," he said simply. "But I can promise I won't ever shut you out. I can handle it differently next time. If there ever is a next time."

But if he spiraled, he wouldn't be responsible for the promises he made now. Sighing, she turned away. "I just don't know if I can handle being ignored and shut out, Elliot. I don't know if I can commit to you now and hope you never leave me again."

"Then let's make a plan," he said, scooting closer to her on the seat. Elliot peeled off the gloves and tucked them under his leg before reaching for her hands. His were still cold, but not as stiff, which was a good sign. His eyes pleaded with her as he spoke. "Give me a chance. I have to go back to LA for a year and finish out my contract with *My Crazy Family*. We can try long-distance for a while and see how it goes."

That did not sound enjoyable in the least. Mia's face must have portrayed her feelings for Elliot scooted even closer. He was right up next to her now and his fingers squeezed her own. "I realize how that sounds. I know long-distance isn't fun. But it'll go so fast. By this time next year my contract will be up, and I can leave the show and move home."

"I need to think about it," Mia said.

Elliot's eyes lit up. "So you're not saying no?"

Mia chuckled, her heart warming despite her reservations. "I'm not saying no."

"You're saying maybe."

She nodded, though she could not ignore the unease that tugged at her stomach. "Yes. I'm saying maybe."

A grin spread over Elliot's lips, his smile wide and inviting. His hands dropped hers, sliding up the puffy arms of her coat and sending shivers down her spine. His gaze fell to her lips and her heart started beating faster than a snowmobile motor as he leaned in close. Elliot's lips were only a breath away from hers, his warmth reaching out and soothing her, and she grew eager with anticipation.

A buzzing sounded just beyond the trees, and Mia stilled. It was an *actual* snowmobile motor, and it was coming toward them. Elliot must have heard the same thing, for he paused. Sighing, he cast her a rueful glance and slid back on the seat.

Mia blew out a breath of pent up energy and watched it cloud before her as Brandon appeared through the trees. She pulled on her helmet to hide her guilty face and turned the ignition, revving up her own snowmobile.

She felt a void behind her and glanced over her shoulder to find Elliot getting off the back.

"My hands are warmed enough," he explained, reaching forward to give her gloves back. "I can drive down now."

Mia nodded, afraid her voice would sound raspy or fail if she tried to use it.

Brandon paused in front of them. "Everything okay?"

"Yeah," Elliot called. "Snowmobile trouble. But we've got it worked out."

Brandon clearly didn't believe him if his sideways glance was any indication. "Good," he said. "I just came up to see if you needed help. But we need to get back."

"Why?" Elliot asked.

Brandon glanced at Mia and then back to his brother-in-law. "Because the bridge is fixed, and the entire Caldwell clan just showed up."

CHAPTER FIFTEEN

Mia had never felt so overwhelmed and underprepared in her entire life. She arrived at the lodge to the chaos of Hannah and Ashlyn checking everyone into their rooms, while simultaneously working with Mrs. Bruin at the front desk to rebook her flight from Salt Lake City to Seattle so she could make it home by Christmas.

Which, incidentally, was tomorrow.

Ashlyn glanced up from the front desk, her eyes wide as Mia approached.

"Is everyone situated?" Mia asked.

"Almost," Ashlyn said, shooting Mrs. Bruin a wide smile where the woman waited on the plush chairs beside the fireplace. "The bridge opened up and the Caldwell family was the first to come through."

"How could they have known it was almost fixed?" Mia asked, whispering.

Ashlyn shrugged, leaning closer. "I assume they were already in Park City waiting it out. But we've got their rooms ready so it's fine."

What a relief. Mia checked over the reservations to ensure

herself everyone was placed in their proper rooms, and it all checked out. Ashlyn and Hannah had done their jobs well.

Mia had passed Elliot's aunt and uncle in the hallway with his grandpa, but none of them had recognized her. It wasn't so odd; she'd only met them a handful of times. But she was not looking forward to running into his—

"Mia Murphy?" a high-pitched voice called across the lobby.

Well, nothing she could do about it now. She lifted her gaze to find Mrs. James cross the foyer toward her, a shocked expression on her pale face.

"Hello," Mia called.

"It *is* you!" Mrs. James said, and Mia laughed awkwardly. She stepped out from behind the desk and was immediately pulled into a strong embrace. "Oh, honey. It's been years! What are you doing here?"

"I work here," Mia said, indicating the nametag on her blouse. "I've been at Powder Peaks about eight months now. I had no idea this was the lodge your family used for Christmas, Mrs. James."

"It's a more recent tradition," Mrs. James said. "And please, call me Sylvia. You aren't in high school anymore."

"No, I certainly am not," Mia agreed. "I'm acting manager during your stay, so please reach out to me if there is anything you find yourself in need of."

"Well our stay has been cut dramatically short," Sylvia said. "But I would love it if we could rearrange some of our planned activities to really pack a punch today and tomorrow."

Dread filled Mia's stomach. She'd used up all of the supplies for sugar cookie decorating, and the cranberries for their Christmas dinner was gone. The guests had already caroled and watched movies...but perhaps they wouldn't mind repeating some of these things for the sake of their mother.

"I must inform you," Mia said, affecting her most professional demeanor, "that we utilized some of the supplies for your activities while the guests of the lodge were snowed in. If you can pinpoint precisely what changes you'd like to make to the schedule, however, I will do my best to make it happen."

Sylvia's face did not alter one bit. She smiled pleasantly. "Don't concern yourself too much, Mia. I just wanted to decorate cookies with my grandkids and then maybe take over the parlor for a while tonight to sing carols. Have you done either of those activities?"

Both. Mia nodded. "Yes, but I am sure they won't mind doing them again now that their family has arrived. In fact…" An idea dawned on Mia, and she glanced over her shoulder where Ashlyn sat on the phone speaking to a representative from the airport. "If you can give me a few minutes to speak to our chef then I might be able to change it up a little for the kids. Would you mind if they aren't sugar cookies?"

"Not at all," Sylvia said at once. "We just want to spend time together."

As a family holiday ought to be.

"In the meantime," Sylvia continued, "do you know if the projector is around and working? I've brought a few movies."

"It is," Mia said. "And I can get that set up right away. Give me about twenty minutes, and I'll have the sofas carried into the Wasatch Room and the projector set up."

"Lovely." Sylvia turned to go but paused. Coming back to face Mia, she reached forward and pulled her into another hug, squeezing tightly. "It is so nice to see you again. What a lovely holiday surprise."

The warm reception wasn't entirely surprising, but gratifying nonetheless. Mia had missed this family, and aside from Elliot, she'd missed Sylvia most of all.

The front door opened and a gust of wind blew in, followed directly by a gorgeous, tall redhead with a long, white coat and perfect, bright red lipstick.

It was Sophy Grant.

Sophy Grant turned and caught Mia's eye a moment before her gaze flicked about the room, disgust and annoyance on her brow.

Mia's stomach did a somersault. There was only one reason a high-profile TV star would step foot in her lobby right this moment, and he had just asked Mia to be his girlfriend.

Tearing her gaze away from the most beautiful woman she'd ever seen in real life, Mia cleared her throat. "I might need more like thirty minutes, Sylvia."

Sylvia nodded, glancing between Mia and Sophy before heading for the elevator.

"Hello?" Sophy Grant called, an obnoxious whine to her voice. "Can I get a little help here?"

The woman was standing on the rug just inside the doors. She had no bags except a tiny backpack hanging over one shoulder. What could she possibly need help with?

Mia glanced to Ashlyn and found her wide-eyed and open-mouthed. The phone was still against Ashlyn's ear and someone must have spoken to her, because she snapped out of her trance and began talking into the phone again, but her gaze didn't leave the red-headed supermodel.

Mia crossed the lobby, pulling off her hat and shoving it into her coat pocket. "Hello, what can I do for you?" It was on the tip of her tongue to ask if the woman needed help checking in, but since Mia hoped that wasn't the case, she didn't offer.

Sophy Grant turned narrowed eyes on her, glancing up and down Mia's unprofessional snow gear. "I'm looking for someone. Can you tell me if Elliot James is here?"

Mia's stomach fell. Of course she *assumed* that was Sophy Grant's purpose for being in Hidden Hollow, but hearing the words solidified her fears. Was there more between them than Elliot had led her to believe? "I am sorry, but it is against hotel policy to reveal any information about our guests. I'm sure you understand."

"No, I don't. I'm Sophy Grant and all of America knows that I have a personal relationship with Elliot James. Now, I don't want to stand around in this cabin for longer than I need to. Please inform Elliot that I'm here right away."

Mia clenched her jaw. It was against hotel policy to tell Sophy Grant anything, but she could call up to Elliot's room and let him know he had a guest waiting for him. "If you would like to be seated, I will see what I can do."

Sophy turned away, clicking her heels across the lobby before she dropped daintily into a plush armchair. The chair was likely covered in dog hair since Mrs. Bruin and Snookums had recently vacated it, which only caused Mia to smile.

"Your car will arrive within fifteen minutes and drive you straight to the airport," Ashlyn was saying to Mrs. Bruin when Mia went behind the desk.

"Wonderful," Mrs. Bruin said. "Thank you for all you've done this week."

"We are happy to have been part of your holiday, Mrs. Bruin," Mia said. "But we are also glad we can get you back to Seattle by Christmas."

"Just barely," Mrs. Bruin said. "But we've done it."

Mia lifted the phone and dialed the extension to Elliot's room while Ashlyn printed out the forms for Mrs. Bruin's checkout.

A sudden gasp ripped from Mrs. Bruin, causing Mia to jump where she stood. "That is Sophy Grant," Mrs. Bruin said with reverence, her eyes wide in delight. "*The* Sophy Grant is sitting in this lobby. Oh my heavens. Do you think she's here for Elliot James?"

"Hello?" Elliot's voice rang through the receiver. Mia was stunned momentarily. "Hello?" he repeated.

"Yes, hello. It's Mia Murphy, the assistant manager."

Elliot chuckled and the sound was like warm honey. "What's up?"

"Um," Mia said, looking between Mrs. Bruin and Ashlyn.

Mrs. Bruin leaned in closer. "You don't think old women like television? I'll let you in on a secret: we do." She cackled and Ashlyn laughed politely.

The elevator doors opened and Hannah stepped out, pausing halfway across the lobby when her sights landed on the celebrity in the armchair.

"Mia, are you still there?"

"I'm sorry," she said quickly. "It's kind of crazy down here right now. Listen," Mia said, turning away from the lobby and leaning back against the counter, "there is a woman here who would like me to summon you. I've explained that I can't give out guest's information, but she's adamant...she needs to see you."

The line was silent.

"Elliot?"

"Yeah, I'm here. Is it Sophy?"

"Yes," Mia confirmed, her voice sounding as strained as she felt. She hoped he wouldn't pick up on that.

Elliot sighed into the phone. "I'm sorry, Mia. I just got out of the shower so it'll take me a minute to get dressed, but I'll be down as quickly as I can."

"I'll let her know."

Mia hung up the phone and directed her attention to Hannah, who was still frozen in place. She hoped the employee would have enough sense to come to the front desk and avoid approaching Sophy Grant, but the brunette seemed undecided.

"I am probably their biggest fan," Mrs. Bruin said. "I was rooting for them to get together, but the tabloids only had those same few photos over and over again. So if they *were* dating, they were probably very discreet."

Mia's stomach grew sicker the more she listened.

"Well," Mrs. Bruin said with a bright smile, "I suppose I ought to ask the woman for an autograph since I will probably never have this opportunity again. Or perhaps I should ask for a selfie?"

Hearing the word selfie from Mrs. Bruin's lips was as incongruent with the woman as learning about her abiding love for *My Crazy Family*.

But she was not a hotel employee, and she was no longer a guest, so Mia could not do anything about Mrs. Bruin approaching Sophy Grant. Instead, she sat back and watched.

She could inform the TV star about Elliot's impending arrival right after Mrs. Bruin got her selfie.

Hannah stepped behind the desk and plopped into the chair beside Ashlyn. "I don't know about you guys, but this has been a weird week."

Ashlyn nodded. "Seriously."

Both of their gazes were trained on the short, white-haired woman pulling along a terrier on a thin, red leash and approaching a bored looking television star.

Mia joined them in watching.

They couldn't hear Mrs. Bruin from where they sat, but it was obvious when she'd asked for the photo, for Sophy Grant gave the woman a short, tight smile and stood, smiling into the camera while Mrs. Bruin held it at arm's length.

The moment Mrs. Bruin lowered her phone, Sophy Grant's face fell back into a flat, irritated expression, and she sat in the chair. Mrs. Bruin said something to her, and she nodded back.

The front door opened and Ashlyn's brother, Jacob, stepped inside. He was utilized by the lodge occasionally to drive people to or from the airport and was compensated by Janice for the job.

Hannah shot to her feet. "I'll let Mrs. Bruin know her ride is here."

She was out from behind the counter before Mia could respond. "How did she even know Jacob was here for Mrs. Bruin?"

"She knew Mrs. Bruin was heading to the airport, so it wasn't much of a stretch," Ashlyn said. "The better question is why you double booked us today to work the front desk."

"I didn't," Mia said. She sat at the computer and pulled up the schedule, but it was only Ashlyn's name which filled the spot for Christmas Eve. "In fact, she isn't on the schedule at all this week. She requested it off for a family vacation."

"She was stuck in town like the rest of us," Ashlyn said, her tone dripping in irritation. "I bet her trip was canceled. And I bet she's only here for more Elliot sightings."

"Probably," Mia agreed.

Jacob crossed toward the desk and picked up Mrs. Bruin's suitcase and dog carrier. "I'm guessing these go?" he asked.

"Yep," Ashlyn said. "And hey, when you get home can you tell Mom not to bother with the eggnog today? I can make it when I get off work."

Jacob nodded before carrying the items outside. When he came back into the lobby, Mrs. Bruin was waiting by the door. She sent them a little wave and Mia and Ashlyn both waved back.

Hannah was sitting in the chair beside Sophy Grant, her face an awed mix of excitement and bewilderment.

The door to the stairwell opened and Elliot stepped out. He looked around the lobby, his gaze passing over Sophy Grant and landing on Mia.

He grimaced. He shot her an apologetic look and crossed the lobby.

Sophy stood as soon as she saw the man she came for. She closed the distance between them and threw her arms around Elliot's neck.

Mia wanted to throw up.

She turned away. "I've got to talk to Rosie and set up the projector for the Caldwell family in the Wasatch Room. You've got things under control here?"

Ashlyn nodded, her eyes glued to the reunion.

"Then I'm out," Mia said. She glanced back at them once and found Elliot leading Sophy away, her arm grasping his as though he supported her entirely. Shuddering, Mia swallowed her disappointment and walked from the room.

CHAPTER SIXTEEN

E lliot peeled Sophy off of his neck. "Should we go into the parlor over here?"

Sophy nodded, stringing her arm through Elliot's as he led her away.

"What's going on?" He closed the parlor door and led her to a set of chairs. "Why did you come all the way to Utah?"

"You haven't been watching the news?" Sophy asked, arching her eyebrow in superiority.

"No."

"Well, surely Frank has kept you informed, right?"

Elliot swallowed his irritation, pulling his arm from her grip. "I've ignored his calls and texts. Sophy, it's Christmas Eve. What could be so important that you'd come all the way here?"

She pierced him with a glare. "Hansen has been arrested. He was caught selling drugs to minors, and they found a whole sales ring among the producers, so the show is off."

"Off?"

"Yeah, totally done." Sophy's face broke into tears. "We're *canceled*, Elliot."

His heart leapt in his chest. "For good?"

"If you bothered to check in with your agent I'm sure you'd find a termination agreement somewhere in his email."

"That's great," Elliot said, sitting on the arm of the sofa. "I'm done."

"What is great about being canceled?" Sophy wailed. "This is absolutely horrible. You need to come back to LA with me and talk some sense into Tommy and Mark. Just because Hansen was arrested doesn't mean the entire show has to go off."

"I don't want to talk sense into Tommy or Mark. And they wouldn't listen to me anyway. I'm done, Sophy. I'm quitting."

"You can't quit," she all but screeched. "I need this show, Elliot. We can't get canceled mid-season. Who would pick us up?"

"I don't want to be picked up," Elliot said. Again. All he wanted in that moment was to go find Mia and share his news. Maybe their long-distance didn't need to be quite so distanced after all. "I'm not coming back to LA, Sophy. I'm going to sign my termination agreement and walk away. If you want to get the show back up, you should try getting help from Alex or Sam."

Sophy glared at him. And he understood immediately. She'd dated their other coworkers, both Alex and Sam, and none of them got along anymore.

"You could try Angelica," he offered. "She might have a connection to someone over at the CW. I heard her mention it once."

Sophy perked up, her eyes lighting. "That's true, huh? She always talked about her stupid step-dad and his friend at CW." Grasping his shoulders, Sophy leaned down and gave him a kiss on the cheek. "Elliot, you're brilliant. *Ciao*, babe."

Sophy spun away, leaving the parlor, her heels clicking across the lobby and straight out the door. He was sure her car had idled right on Main Street for the duration of their conversation.

He pulled his phone from his pocket and went straight to his voicemail. There were a dozen messages from Frank, his agent, and he listened to them all. His grin widened as the messages altered from Frank trying to convince him to agree to the commercial, to Frank calmly explaining what Sophy had said, only carefully choosing his words so as not to make the situation sound as dire as it was. Frank knew that Elliot wanted out. It was probably why the agent hadn't mentioned a termination agreement at all.

Dialing Frank's number, Elliot held the phone to his ear and waited.

"Finally," Frank answered. "I began to wonder if you died."

"I'm alive, and I just had an interesting visit from my red-headed co-star."

Frank cursed. "She wants you to try and get the show picked up by a different network, doesn't she?"

"Yes. And I'm not doing it, Frank. I'm out. I want you to email me the termination agreement so I can sign it and be done."

"Just listen to reason, Elliot—"

"No. I'm done. You know how long I've wanted to be done, Frank, so don't even bother trying to convince me otherwise. Send me the forms so I can sign them and enjoy the rest of Christmas with my family. And then do me a favor."

"What?" Frank asked, his voice sad and sullen.

"Go enjoy Christmas with your own family."

Silence sat on the line between them, followed by a sigh. "I'll send the forms now."

"Thanks, Frank. Merry Christmas," Elliot said.

"Bah."

Frank clicked off and Elliot lowered his phone, checking his email repeatedly until the forward came through. He scanned the document and then opened the e-sign program and swiped his finger across the screen in a semblance of a signature.

And all at once, the weight fell off his shoulders and tumbled to the rug at his feet. He was done. He was free.

He could move back to Utah.

He could be with Mia.

As the thoughts settled in his mind, his smile grew wider and wider. He slid his phone into his pocket and left the parlor. He needed to find Mia now.

Rosie had agreed to make little gingerbread men for the kids to decorate while Mia walked to the market down the street and found sprinkles to replenish the stash she'd used up for the sugar cookies.

The projector was set up and Hannah left in charge of orchestrating the movie for the Caldwells and getting the sofas moved into the Wasatch Room once Elliot and Sophy Grant vacated the parlor.

Everything was working out fine. Even seeing Sylvia James after all those years hadn't been as difficult as Mia had expected it to be. It was much the opposite, like a warm reunion.

Slipping out the front doors, Mia passed a shiny black Range Rover parallel parked in front of the hotel. The windows were tinted, and the driver looked bored—most likely Sophy Grant's vehicle.

Mia huffed and her breath formed a cloud in front of her. She walked through it and tried to ease the scowl on her forehead. She hadn't expected to see one TV star in their lobby this week, let alone two. Janice had no idea just how involved this week was going to be when she left her hotel in Mia's hands, and if Mia hadn't proved herself yet, she was unlikely to ever do so.

The market was at the other end of the block, and Mia reached it in a few minutes. Gathering all of the holiday sprinkles they had available, Mia threw them into her basket along with gumdrops and red hots.

She paused near the checkout stall. There was a stand of canned cranberry sauce, so she picked up a few cans and added them to her basket. It wasn't anything like the fresh sauce, but canned was better than nothing. Once everything was bagged up, Mia wished the clerk a Merry Christmas and headed back into the cold.

She was halfway back to the hotel when she remembered that she was nearly out of dog food. Pug had been a champ the last few days hanging out in the hotel room and down under the front desk in reception. Mia made a mental note to get him one of those squeaky bones he loved so much when they were back at home.

She walked down the sidewalk, doing her very best to think of Pug and how she would reward him and not the handsome TV star who was probably introducing another gorgeous TV star to his family right about now.

It was fine that Sophy went back to Elliot. It just proved that getting back together with him was obviously a bad idea for Mia.

At least she hadn't kissed him on that snowmobile.

"Mia!"

She paused on the sidewalk. She knew that voice, and it belonged to Elliot.

"Mia, hold on," he yelled again.

Mia glanced over her shoulder and found him jogging down the sidewalk toward her. Alone.

His cheeks were red, and his nose was turning pink from the cold.

"You've really got to quit going outside without proper attire," she said. "You aren't in LA right now."

He nodded. "Yeah, I know. But I wasn't expecting to chase

you down outside. I was hoping you were in the nice, warm lodge setting up the movie thing for my mom."

"Hannah's taking care of that."

He lifted his eyebrows. "Imagine my disappointment when I discovered that. The girl has been grilling my mom about what I was like as a kid."

Mia couldn't help but smile. "If it's any consolation, she'll probably get written up for it."

"No, don't do that," Elliot said. "I don't really care. She's harmless."

Mia adjusted the grocery bag in her hand. "What do you need, Elliot?" she asked, her voice sounding as tired as she felt.

"You."

The bag slipped from her hand and dropped on the wet, salty sidewalk.

Elliot took a step closer. "I want you, Mia."

She began to shake her head, glancing over his shoulder to where the Range Rover was parked on the street. But it was gone. "Where is Sophy Grant?"

"I don't know, probably heading toward the airport."

Mia reached down and picked up the grocery bag. "Elliot, don't play games with me."

"I'm not," he said, moving closer. "She's gone."

"Why did she come at all, then?"

"To persuade me to come back to LA and convince another network to pick up our show."

"Why would—"

"We've been canceled," he said, grinning. "*My Crazy Family* is over."

Mia didn't understand why he was so thrilled about being fired. Or why Sophy would come all the way to a town just outside of Park City, Utah to drag him away from his family on Christmas Eve. "Why is that a good thing?"

"Because then I can stay here with you."

Her eyebrows lifted of their own accord. "You're moving to Hidden Hollow?"

Elliot's gaze flicked away. He scuffed his shoe against the ground as though he was bashful, which was entirely new for him. "I want to be with you, Mia. I want to erase the last six years and start over. I want to come back to Utah to be closer to my family and to scrap the entertainment industry altogether." He sucked in a lung full of air and blew it out, his cheeks puffing up. "I think I want to teach kids how to snowboard. Or teenagers. I don't know. I liked instructing today, and I feel like I could be good at it."

"Have you been on a snowboard yet?" She meant since the accident, but she felt like Elliot understood.

"No. But I can do it. I just might take it easy and avoid the half pipes until I'm a little more comfortable."

Mia smiled. She couldn't help it. "I think that sounds great, Elliot."

He nodded, his face growing serious. "I really feel like my life's coming together. And even if I don't come to Hidden Hollow, I could get a job in Park City and only be twenty minutes away."

Mia shook her head. "Elliot, this all sounds great and everything, but you've got your vacation goggles on. It's not realistic."

"My *what*?"

"Your vacation goggles. You know, like you are seeing everything through a different lens because you're on vacation. Actually quitting the show and closing out your house in LA and saying goodbye to the people there won't be easy. Plus, you have to actually get a job here and then move. And if you move *here*, you're still an hour and a half away from your parents' house. So it's not like you'll be seeing them all the time."

"Let's drop the realism for a moment, okay?" Elliot said. "Yes, that will all take time and work, but give me a month, and

I can make it happen. Do you know what I think is really happening?" he asked, his voice growing serious.

Mia shook her head.

"I think you're coming up with any excuse to keep us apart. I think you're scared to say yes to me because you're afraid I'll turn around and leave. Just like you automatically assumed Sophy was here to get back together with me. And you know what? Even if she had been—which is ludicrous—I wouldn't have taken her back. Because I want you, Mia. I've only ever wanted you."

He'd hit on the problem so astutely that Mia was afraid to say anything. She *was* scared. And she had a right to be. "How can I know it won't happen again?" she asked him again, repeating her question from their conversation on the snowmobile.

"This is where you've just got to trust, Mia. Trust in us." He stepped forward and reached for her hand. "Trust *me*."

She let out a shuddering breath and Elliot pulled her forward, wrapping her in a warm, comfortable embrace. She hadn't expected to see him when she agreed to take on managing the lodge for the week, but she was fairly sure now that even if she had known everything that was going to happen, she still would have accepted the job.

Because Elliot was right. She'd already forgiven him, and she already knew she still had strong feelings for him. What she needed to come to terms with was the distinct possibility that he could succumb to his situational depression again.

It wasn't something she understood firsthand, but she could learn. If he could be open.

"If I agree to this crazy scheme," she said, pulling away from him, "then you have to agree to go to counseling with me."

The look on his face betrayed his surprise.

"There is nothing wrong with using a professional to help us have healthy conversations. You don't have to be having problems to see a counselor."

"I know," Elliot said, raising his hands. "I didn't say no. I'm just surprised by the request."

"And it's not negotiable. I know nothing about depression, Elliot. But if it ever happens again, I want to be prepared to help you in the best way I can."

A slow smile spread across his face. "You know what you sound like?"

"What?" she asked, trying to keep her own expression flat.

"It sounds like you decided to trust me."

The pure joy on Elliot's face was hard to ignore, and Mia found her own heart radiating in turn. "Don't make me regret it," she said.

"Never." Elliot wrapped his arms around her, pulling her close. Her hands rested on his arms while he rubbed his nose against hers like he used to do in high school.

"Mia Murphy, I love you."

She thought her chest was going to explode from the joy she felt hearing those words. She tilted her head up to look him in the eye. "Yeah, I think I'm fond of you, too."

"You're still such a tease," Elliot said and closed the space, bringing his lips to hers and kissing her with all of the pent-up energy he'd likely been holding in all week. His kiss was infused with the magic of old and new combining into one, the familiar way he tasted and felt, only aged in a pleasant way.

Someone whistled from down the sidewalk, and they broke apart to find Brandon down by the hotel, crossing the road to retrieve something from his car.

"We better get back inside," Elliot said. "My mom brought *The Christmas Story*."

"I have to run back to the store to get more dog food for Pug."

Elliot took the bag of sprinkles from Mia and cocked an

eyebrow, sliding his free hand into hers as they walked back to the market. "Don't you mean *the* pug. What's his name?"

"His name is Pug." She could tell Elliot was confused. "You know in *Breakfast at Tiffany's* how Audrey Hepburn's character calls her cat Cat? I've always wanted to do that. So when I got a pug, I named him Pug."

Elliot chuckled, releasing her hand to reach for the door and hold it open for her. "You've always been weird about old movies."

"Because they're the best. Watch what you say, or I'll make you watch some really old ones with me. There's quite a few Christmas movies made before nineteen-fifty that rock, you know."

Elliot leaned down and stole a quick kiss. "Hey, I'm not complaining. I'll watch anything with you."

CHAPTER SEVENTEEN

Christmas had come and gone and both the Kirkpatrick and the Caldwell families had left the lodge, replaced by new guests. Mia was checking each suite for things left behind in drawers and under beds but reached the last room and came up empty.

The staff at the Powder Peaks Lodge really was top notch. And if Sylvia James's glowing review on Yelp counted for anything, then Janice was going to be pleased when she returned from Arizona that evening.

Her phone buzzed, and she pulled it from her pocket. There was a text from Ashlyn.

There's a package down at reception for you.

Mia slid her phone back into her pocket and left the suite, making her way toward the elevator to ride down to the main floor.

Once she reached the lobby, Ashlyn glanced up and smiled. "I don't know what's in it, but it's leaking all over the desk."

"What?" Mia jogged the remainder of the way and recognized the familiar scrawl at once. It was the package from her mom. Ripping the box open, she started laughing.

"What's in it?" Ashlyn asked, rising to peek into the box.

"Gingerbread and eggnog. But I think the eggnog carton opened somehow because it leaked everywhere."

"And judging by the smell, it wasn't refrigerated."

Mia picked up a trash bin from the floor and slid the whole package into it. No wonder her mother had requested that she opened it up right away.

She was rummaging in the supply closet for paper towels and cleaning solution when she heard a familiar voice in the lobby and her heart stopped. It was time.

Hurrying back to the front desk, Mia brandished a wide smile on her face and set the supplies on the desk before crossing the floor to meet her boss.

"Janice," she said pleasantly, "welcome home. How was your flight?"

"Too long," Janice said. Her spiky white hair and bright pink lips looked undisturbed from the travel and her pantsuit was flawless. The woman was a machine. "And interesting. I had a message when I landed from a guest who called to chat about the *service* they received this week."

Mia froze. A guest had called Janice? Who would have known her well enough to have her personal cell phone number?

"She had interesting things to say about how the rooms were handled after the bridge was damaged. And something about various activities."

Janice peered at her through indifferent eyes, and Mia could not decipher if she was pleased or angry.

She swallowed. "After we were snowed in, I took it upon myself to create activities to keep the guests from growing too bored or uncomfortable. And there was one guest who was meant to leave but couldn't, due to circumstances out of her control, so I comped her room until she was able to get past the bridge."

"And then organized a free ride to the airport?" Janice asked with one sleek, white eyebrow raised in question.

"Yes," Mia said. She wasn't going to apologize for what she had done for Mrs. Bruin. The poor woman was stuck at a lodge when she wanted to be home. It was the least she could do.

"Well," Janice said, her face unreadable. "I say well done."

Mia stood in front of her boss, dumbfounded.

"Elizabeth Bruin is an old friend of mine. She comes out here every year around Christmas to see me and we spend some time together before she goes back to Seattle. When I decided to go to my daughter's house for the holidays this year, I asked Elizabeth if she was interested in coming out as planned and being my little fly on the wall."

"You spied on me," Mia said, understanding.

"Well, yes. I suppose so. But I wasn't worried. I just wanted to know how you would handle certain situations while I was gone. And according to Elizabeth's report, you did a fantastic job."

"Did you orchestrate everything?"

"Of course not," Janice said, laughing. "I didn't create the avalanche or damage the bridge. But those ended up working out in my favor so I got to see how you would handle guests under duress."

"No one was under duress," Mia explained.

"No, but they could have been. Being snowed in on Main Street in our tiny little town could cause some people to grow overwhelmed and claustrophobic. But you handled everything so well and kept the guests busy and their mind off of the problem until the problem was fixed. It was precisely what I would have done." Janice tilted her head. "And it is precisely why I do not have any problem offering you a promotion to manager."

Mia gasped. "You're stepping back?"

"Just a little," Janice said. "I'll still be around a lot. But I'm passing off the official reins, and we can run the lodge together."

Mia stepped forward and pulled Janice into a hug. She couldn't be thrilled that Janice had chosen to test her in such a way, but she'd passed. She was now the manager.

"What about the chocolate cake?" Mia asked when she released her boss. "Was there a reason she only asked for it a few nights and then stopped?"

Janice chuckled. "I asked her to do that. I wanted to know if you'd go above and beyond for a guest. I didn't anticipate that you'd have to go above and beyond for the duration of my absence, or I wouldn't have devised the cake thing."

Mia shook her head and left to clean the eggnog from the desk. She finished wiping up the remnants and tossed the paper towels in the trash when her phone rang. The lobby was empty, so she pulled it out to see who was calling.

Elliot.

She answered the phone and began gathering the supplies to return to the closet.

"Hey," she said.

"Hey," he said back. "I just got to my apartment. I don't think I'm gonna bother packing. I think I'll just donate everything I own and buy all new things again in Utah."

"No, don't donate anything," Mia argued. "Sell it all on eBay. Then you'll raise enough to buy even better stuff when you come to Utah."

"Should I autograph everything, too?" Elliot asked, amusement lacing his tone. "I could take a sharpie to all my furniture and picture frames really fast."

Mia mocked affront. "I know you're teasing, but people would pay good money for that." She paused, her voice thoughtful. "You know, in all honesty, it's not such a bad idea."

Elliot chuckled. "I think I'll stick with paying movers to deal with all of it."

"Once you have an apartment," Mia reminded him, crossing the lobby toward the plush chairs.

"Actually," Elliot said, drawing out the word. "I just might have found a place to live."

Mia froze, dropping into a chair.

"You know that cabin-looking house between Hidden Hollow and Park City?"

"The one with the red painted door?" Of course she knew that house. It was set back from the road enough for privacy, but close enough to be easily accessible. And it was so cute.

"Yeah, that one. I might have bought it."

Excitement bubbled up in Mia's chest and threatened to spill out in the form of a squeal. "Seriously?"

"Yes," Elliot said, very pleased with himself. "Seriously."

"You'll be so close to me."

"And close enough to Park City to make the commute a breeze, even in the winter."

"I could kiss you right now," Mia said.

Elliot whined. "I should have waited to tell you in person."

"I'm glad you didn't. So when do you come back?"

"I've got to wrap up some loose ends here, but I was thinking Saturday. I've got to wait until the house closes to move in, so I think I'll go down and spend some time with my parents until then."

"Hey, Saturday is when I go down to spend a few days with *my* parents," Mia said facetiously.

"Fancy that. Mind if I hitch a ride?"

Mia couldn't help but smile. "No, Elliot. I don't mind at all."

"Hey Mia?"

"Yeah?"

"I sure love you."

Mia's heart filled near to bursting. "I sure love you, too."

EPILOGUE

E lliot had planned everything perfectly for a classic movie marathon. He checked the clock and sucked in a breath. Mia was going to arrive any moment and the DVD player chose *now* to quit working. Frustrated, he unplugged the whole TV, counted to ten, and then restarted everything.

A soft knock came at the front door, and it opened. "I'm here," Mia called. Yapping followed behind her and Pug ran up to Elliot, jumping onto his lap where he sat on the floor.

Mia put a few bags of takeout down on the counter and turned toward Elliot. "The bartender at Hal's eyed my ring tonight," she said, flashing her hand. "Maybe he'll quit hitting on me now."

"You mean my requests weren't enough, but that ring might be?" Elliot asked, skeptically.

Mia beamed. "I don't even care. I just walked around all day waving my hand so everyone can admire my rock with me. Hey, I've got an idea," she said, turning toward him. "What do you think about a Christmas wedding? And we can do it at the lodge."

Elliot chuckled, rising carefully while Pug jumped from his lap. He approached his fiancé and wrapped his arms around her. "I don't care where we have it as long as no one knows."

"Except our family."

"Family is welcome, the press is not."

Mia nodded in agreement. "You know, I was kidding, but it's not actually that bad of an idea. We could do it on Christmas Eve, and you know Janice won't care if we have it at the lodge. All of your family would be there anyway for the holiday, so we'd just have to make sure there's room for mine."

"And if not," Elliot added, "your family could stay in your apartment. Because now that we're getting married you could finally move in here."

Mia's eyes lit up. "And then I finally get to decorate."

Elliot chortled, a snort escaping through his nose. "Excuse me? What do you call all of that?" He gestured to the many things Mia had added to his house since he'd moved in the January before.

"Gifts," she said with a straight face. "But you wouldn't complain about my adding a little touch here and there, right? Especially if we're going to make this our home."

Elliot rested his hands on either side of Mia's face. "You can do whatever you'd like to this place as long as you're living in it with me."

"Deal," Mia agreed.

Elliot leaned forward and kissed her. Pulling back, he gave her nose an Eskimo kiss. "Let's do it. Let's get married on Christmas Eve."

Mia squealed. "Who'd have thought it, huh? This time last year I didn't even want to see your face."

"I believe you used the words, 'I'd rather get run over by Santa's sleigh than—"

"Yeah, yeah. I remember."

Elliot picked up the takeout bags and took them into the kitchen to put the food on plates. "Aren't you glad you decided to trust?"

Mia followed him into the kitchen, reaching up to place a kiss on his cheek. "More than you know."

MELODIES AND MISTLETOE
SNEAK PEEK: CHAPTER ONE

Hailey Grant scooped up the pile of stuffed animals on the plush living room rug and balanced them close to her chest so she would only have to take one trip upstairs to deliver the things to the toy bin. A dotted ladybug toppled from the pile and rolled across the stark white rug, landing under the fake, snow-tipped branches of the Christmas tree.

Ugh. Gently crouching, Hailey reached for the ladybug and set it on top of the pile in her arms before slowly standing again, her thighs burning. Sheesh. Maybe she needed to add squats to her daily routine. She could slip them in right after her race to get dressed in the morning, shortly before grabbing a granola bar on her way out the door.

Or maybe she could set a new rule for herself: every time she bent to pick up a stuffed animal at work, she would squat. Her butt would look amazing in no time.

Some kids hoarded stuffed animals, collecting them like those spoons people bought in souvenir shops but never intended to use. Those types of kids arranged their stuffed animals pleasantly across their beds without planning to ever play with them. But Kendra was different. Kendra, the six-year-old girl Hailey spent her afternoons chasing around the high-rise New York City loft, played with those little suckers like they were her best friends. And she didn't gravitate toward the type of animals that typically lived on the beds of six-year-olds. No, she loved the *bugs* most.

The fact that they *did* keep her so thoroughly entertained at least made cleaning up what felt like thousands of stuffed bugs every night totally worth it. At least Kendra wasn't into fashion dolls. All those little accessories everywhere would be so much worse.

Hailey paused on the landing at the top of the stairs and peeked through Kendra's open door at the girl's small, sleeping form nestled under the blanket. Oh, please don't ever, *ever* discover fashion dolls.

After the stuffed caterpillars, beetles, and butterflies were all safely stored in the giant bin in the dim room, Hailey took the *Life Cycle of a Butterfly* book perched beside Kendra's pillow and tucked it back onto the bookshelf. She double-checked the latch on the window to make sure it was locked, then let herself quietly out of the room.

Seamless.

It hadn't been this easy in the beginning. Hailey had come to work for the Martinez family when Kendra wasn't even two. It'd been an adjustment, but she'd only meant to nanny for a year or so—however long it took her to get noticed.

But sometimes things didn't work out the way they were so carefully planned. Hailey was *fine* with how her life had turned out so far. She loved Kendra, and the Martinezes paid her insanely well. Of course, her salary was a drop in the barrel that was the immense Martinez fortune. But it was more than enough to keep her stocked in sound equipment and guitar strings. They probably had no idea they were funding such an expensive side hustle.

If moonlighting at bars or producing demos could even be

called a side-hustle. Didn't it have to actually bring in money to earn that title?

The elevator ding rang across the marble floors, and Hailey darted down the stairs, her extra-thick socks padding her silent footsteps. If she hurried, she might make it to Nomad before the band scheduled before her, Midnight Moods, finished their set. And she *had* to be there before they finished, or she was done for. Johnny already told her that if she was late one more time, he'd take her off the docket completely.

But tonight she was prepared. She'd brought her guitar, dressed nice enough for playing in a bar—which, admittedly, wasn't any different from her regular clothes, just a lot more black—and had her Uber app opened and ready to go.

The elevator doors beeped from the Martinezes' foyer before opening, and Amber Martinez stepped into the apartment, her stilettos clicking loudly.

"How was your day?" Hailey asked, sitting on the tufted bench to pull on her boots.

"Fine." Amber waved her hand dismissively. She crossed into the kitchen, visible through the wide, open doorway, and dropped her bag on the center island. "Is Kenny asleep?"

"Yep. She's been out for thirty minutes or so."

Amber nodded. The bags under her eyes and drooping smile highlighted her constant late nights at the office, but she had nothing on her husband. Luis was basically never home.

Hailey leaned down to zip her boots. "Megan had to leave early, so I stacked your laundry in the closet, and she promised to stay late tomorrow."

Amber filled a glass with water from the fridge. "That's fine. I'm sure she'll make up her hours." She glanced over her shoulder, giving Hailey's faded black jeans and boots a once-over. That was all that was visible under the marshmallow-puffy coat Hailey was zipping up. "Where are you heading off to?"

"Just to Nomad." Hailey lifted her guitar case and slung her purse over her shoulder.

Amber's brows lifted. "You've got a gig?"

"I don't know if it qualifies as a gig, but I sing there sometimes."

Amber offered a wan smile. "I want to tell you good luck, but I also never want to lose you."

Hailey used all her self-control to *not* check the time on her phone. She needed to get out of there. And fast. "You know I adore Kendra. It'll take a major recording contract to get me to leave her."

"Good," Amber said. Oddly enough, she sounded super relieved. Thanks for the confidence, boss.

But it was true. Amber had nothing to worry about. The Martinez family wouldn't be losing their nanny anytime soon. Hailey had spent the last four years trying to get her demos into the right hands, and that turned out to be way harder than she'd expected.

"Well, I'll see you tomorrow!" Hailey crossed to the elevator and punched in her key code.

Amber made a farewell-type sound, and Hailey slipped out, hitting the button for the elevator to take her downstairs. Pulse speeding, she wrapped her scarf tighter around her neck and pulled her long, dark curls free. She hitched her bag higher up on her shoulder so she was prepared to run to the corner to meet her Uber driver. This was her last chance to keep the gig and her best shot at being seen. She couldn't lose it.

Declan, the doorman, would give her a scolding tomorrow for running through his lobby, but it'd be worth it. He really was the most crotchety old man sometimes. But hey, he'd been standing sentinel at this building's door for at least a hundred years, so he'd earned himself the right.

A splash of color caught her eye above the doors, and she had to chuckle. Whoever placed mistletoe wrapped in red ribbon up there was clearly a romantic, and it wasn't Amber or Luis. Maybe Declan put it there for a little holiday cheer.

The elevator dinged, and Hailey gripped her guitar tighter, prepared to launch the moment the ancient doors slid open. Light poured through the widening gap as they opened, and Hailey went for it...directly into the man waiting on the other side.

"*Oomph*," he said, taking the brunt of Hailey's guitar case in the chest.

"I'm so sorry!" Hailey backed up, pulling her case flush against her as she turned to keep walking. She didn't have time to waste. "I didn't see you—"

"No, clearly you didn't," he snapped, checking out his suit and only showing her the top of his head. But guitar cases didn't make messes. It might have bruised his nicely sculpted—nope. Hailey shook her head to stop that line of thinking in its tracks. The guy was still looking down, assessing his designer suit, and didn't appear to notice her walking away.

And the faster she escaped, the better. If this guy planned to claim that she'd snagged his Armani sleeve and required a replacement, he had another thing coming. A perfectly fitted suit like that would probably cost her a month's salary—or more —and Hailey wouldn't put it past anyone wearing something that expensive to pull a jerk move like making her pay for a new one. In her experience, people with money tended to have less kindness or basic courtesy. Or maybe it was an overall ignorance? Either way, *clearly* the guy was worried about it, or he wouldn't be analyzing his lapel so closely.

Christmas was only ten days away, so she supposed it made sense that she'd run into a grinch at some point.

"Sorry," she called again, slipping outside into the freezing December air. A glance at her phone made her break out in a run toward the waiting car with the Uber sticker on the back window. Twelve minutes. She had twelve minutes to get to

Nomad or she'd be off the docket. With it being her only connection to music at present, it wasn't something she was willing to give up.

She slid into the car and shut the door, settling the guitar case between her knees.

"Hailey?" the Uber driver asked, catching her eye in the rearview mirror. He matched his ultra-hairy picture the app had given her. Someone needed to get the man some beard oil and a trimmer.

She nodded. "Yes, and I'm in a major hurry."

"Who isn't?" He turned his attention to the road and flipped on his blinker.

Well, great. He really didn't sound like he planned to hurry.

She shut her eyes, leaning her head against the back of the seat rest for about a millisecond before sitting up again. It was an Uber, for heaven's sake. There was no trusting the last person who'd sat in her seat, regardless of how clean the driver was. No lice today, please.

The car absolutely crawled down the street, and Hailey forced herself not to beg the driver to go faster. What man in New York City didn't know how to weave in and out of traffic to his advantage? The amount of space the driver left between his car and the one ahead of them had let so many people in, Hailey was positive she could've run across Central Park faster than it was going to take this guy to drive around it.

All the while, the clock ticked closer and closer to the end of Midnight Moods' set.

She leaned forward and rested her forehead on the guitar case nestled between her knees. It would probably be better to prepare herself for losing the gig completely. Johnny wasn't willing to budge, even a little bit, and she should know—she'd already begged her heart out to get another chance, and this was it. He'd been perfectly clear: if she stepped into the bar one second late, she was out.

Her phone glowed in the back of the dim car, the clock changing. Two minutes left.

Was it pathetic of her to hold on to a dream that wasn't gaining any traction? Defeat closed in on her with each passing second as if the world, covered in twinkle lights and draped in red velvet ribbon, was actually dimming outside the car window like a countdown timer.

By the time the car turned onto Columbus Avenue, Hailey was sunk, her vision nearly void of light. Her last connection to the music world was well and truly severed.

Hailey trudged up three flights of stairs in her ancient apartment building and slid her key into the lock, glaring at the broken elevator over her shoulder. By the time maintenance got around to fixing the elevator—if they ever did—her arms were going to be super toned from lugging groceries and guitars up and down the stairs.

She paused. Well, she wouldn't have to worry about that anymore. At least, not the guitar. Johnny, the manager for Nomad, had ended their agreement and hadn't even had the decency to show a little regret. He wiped her from the docket as easily as he'd swiped away drips of alcohol from the bar top; she was sure she'd seen her career flying away as he'd tossed the used rag over his shoulder. Apparently, Johnny was finished with announcing her act then having to apologize for her tardiness.

She didn't blame him entirely, of course. He had a business to run. But would it have hurt to agree to push the gig back a half-hour?

Hailey pushed the door open and dropped her keys in the

bowl on her entry table, then turned and locked the deadbolt. Colored twinkle lights strung down the hallway cast a rainbow-hued glow over her, and she sighed. She put her things down and rounded the corner into the living room. Nikki had *The Hall-mark Channel* on the television tuned in to one of the Christmas movies, the only lights in the apartment coming from the movie and the twinkle lights strung on the ceiling and wrapped around the tiny tree sitting against the little window. It was a better view than the brick wall they typically got to see from that window, and Nikki had already threatened to keep the tree up all year just to give their apartment some life.

What did it matter if the tree wasn't actually alive? It was green. But they wouldn't need to keep it up. Little did Nikki know, she had some house plants coming her way for Christmas.

"I thought you were playing at Nomad tonight."

"Nope." Hailey slumped onto the battered sofa and dropped her head back. She closed her eyes, tamping down the defeat clawing at her chest. "Johnny fired me. Or he let me go...whatever they call it when they drop you from a job where you don't actually get paid."

"That punk." Nikki sat bolt upright. "Want me to call his mom? I will."

"No." Hailey chuckled. "Your family connections got me the gig, but it was my job to keep it. And it was my fault I lost it. I was late too many times, and he gave me loads of extra chances. It is what it is, I guess."

"You can't just give up. You told him that your boss gets home late all the time, right? You can't just leave Kendra home alone."

"It's fine, Nik." Hailey gave her a side-eye. "It's not like Nomad was actually going to put me on the map."

"It could have. There's a reason their live music spots are so coveted. Johnny said—"

"Yeah, well, he might brag a lot, but none of the reported music execs that supposedly haunt Nomad approached me, like, ever. So I guess I got my answer."

"*Or* you were just unlucky and never played while any of them were there."

Hailey ignored Miss Positivity and turned her attention to the Christmas movie. A man with a lot of hair gel was on his knees, pleading for a woman's forgiveness. Predictable. He'd messed up. She would forgive him. They'd live happily ever after.

Gag.

"Why do you love these movies so much?"

Nikki blinked. "We've gone over this so many times. Because of all the glorious, beautiful hope that good guys still exist."

Hailey fought the urge to roll her eyes and remind her best friend that these were fake, scripted movies. Instead, she snuggled into the sofa, accepting the bowl of popcorn, and watched the show. When it finally came to a blessed end, a song played over the credits, and she closed her eyes, humming along with the music. She harmonized with the indie-sounding woman singing a redone version of *Silent Night, Holy Night*.

When the credits drew to a close, Hailey continued humming, and Nikki picked up the remote, searching the movies for another one to start. If she was hoping to find one she hadn't seen, she was bound to be disappointed.

Hailey hummed the song she would have finished out the set with that night if she hadn't been late—her big finale. It was slower, softer than her usual beats, but so melancholy and beautiful. If she was allowed to think that about something she wrote. There was something she loved about slow, meaningful music, the kind that gave her chills.

"You know what would be cool?" Hailey sat up, the idea coming to her swiftly. "Taking a fast-tempo holiday song and slowing it down."

"Mmhmm," Nikki said, her gaze riveted by the TV and endless carousel of Christmas movie options.

"No, really." Hailey glanced around the apartment until she caught sight of the Christmas tree and her brain gears spun, working and moving until she lit upon the right idea. "Okay, hear me out." She turned to Nikki and started humming *Rocking Around the Christmas Tree*, getting the tune down before adding the words.

Nikki dropped the remote, closing her eyes and listening to the music while Hailey sang. The beat was slow, drawn-out, and almost harrowing. When she finished, she glanced up and paused.

Nikki's wide-eyed gaze was locked on her. "That was cool."

Hailey swallowed. "Too bad I don't have a producer, or I could pitch them my amazing idea."

"Yet," Nikki said. "You don't have a producer *yet*. Do I have to remind you what's taking over half of your bedroom? I'll give you a hint. It's the reason we can't get another roommate in here and maybe save some rent money."

"Don't diss my sound equipment. It's useful stuff. What we really should discuss is why you can't give up half of *your* room to get another roommate in here." Hailey lifted her eyebrows.

Nikki rose. "Moving on..." She went down the hallway and came back with Hailey's guitar case, dropping it in her lap. "I have an idea."

"What?" Hailey shifted the case and clicked it open, her fingers moving on impulse to pull the guitar from its velvet bed.

"Let's record that song and put it on YouTube."

"Uh, no." Hailey laughed. "I doubt it's in the public domain, and I really don't feel like getting sued."

"Okay, scratch that song. We can find another one." She sat down again and pulled out her phone, the screen glowing over her face.

She was crazy. There was no way Hailey was filming herself

and loading the video to YouTube. Nothing screamed pathetic like wannabes trying to get noticed among millions of other people on the internet.

Nikki's eyes lit up. "Ah! What about *Deck the Halls?*"

That one *would* be kind of cool. Plucking a few strings on the guitar, Hailey picked out a tune and moved it down to a minor key. Adding the words was the easy part, and by the time she finished singing the first verse Nikki was actually bouncing in her seat and clapping, a wide smile spread over her freckled face.

"We're going to be famous!"

"We?" Hailey asked.

But Nikki was already up and going into Hailey's room.

She followed. "Whoa, hey, don't touch anything!"

"I'm just moving the chair," Nikki said. She grabbed a stool from the kitchen and put it in front of Hailey's computer. "This is way more indie. Come on, sit."

Hailey obeyed. "I don't know if this is a good idea."

"Eh," Nikki said, shrugging and powering up Hailey's computer. "What harm can it do?" She got everything in order, then turned on the camera app while Hailey fidgeted with her sound equipment. "Ready?"

Hailey probably looked like a deer caught in headlights, because that was exactly how she felt. But Nikki had a point. No one was ever going to see this video. It would sit on YouTube for a hot minute, get zero traction, and she could delete it in the morning when Nikki was at work. Hailey sat back on the stool, lifting her guitar and strumming a few times. "Ready—"

"Wait!" Nikki ran out of the room and returned with a Santa hat, plopping it on Hailey's head and arranging her dark hair over her shoulders. "I'm glad you curled it today. You've got a perfect wave going."

She'd curled it because she thought she'd be on a stage tonight, but that was beside the point.

Stepping back, Nikki rested against the wall and gave her a thumbs up.

Then she pressed start.

The Santa hat drooped to the side a little, but she focused on the chords and the song, allowing her voice and intuition to lead, shoving away all insecurity and doubt. Music had always had a way of wrapping her in a protective hold, pushing negativity and hardship away and letting her breathe. It was therapy for her. It was life.

When it was over, her body tingled, her fingers itching to begin again. Nikki swirled into action, nudging Hailey out of the way, unhooking her computer from the many cords on the desk and taking it to her bed. Hailey watched with growing dread, knots forming in her churning stomach. She pulled down the Santa hat and flung it at her friend. It was so tacky.

Still. It wasn't a problem. She could take the video down in the morning. It was fine. No one would see it.

Nikki finally glanced up, a broad grin on her mouth. "It's live."

Melodies and Mistletoe

She dreams of becoming a famous musician, and he has the ability to make her dreams come true.

She dreams of becoming a famous musician, and he has the ability to make her dreams come true.

ABOUT THE AUTHOR

Kasey Stockton is a staunch lover of all things romantic. She doesn't discriminate between genres and enjoys a wide variety of happily ever afters. Drawn to the Regency period at a young age when gifted a copy of *Sense and Sensibility* by her grandmother, Kasey initially began writing Regency romances. She has since written in a variety of genres, but all of her titles fall under clean romance. A native of northern California, she now resides in Texas with her own prince charming and their three children. When not reading, writing, or binge-watching chick flicks, she enjoys running, cutting hair, and anything chocolate.

Made in United States
Troutdale, OR
11/21/2023

14802194R00105